"We start with the bride."

The dean nodded at Tessa, and she hoped her answering smile looked better than it felt.

"You stand in front of me, dear." He looked up at Isaac expectantly. "Could you stand in as groom for now?"

"Oh, no!" cried Tessa. And everybody looked at her curiously. This twist of fate was just too cruel. Silently she pleaded to Isaac. *I can't bear this. Please refuse. It's not necessary.*

Isaac's eyes bored into her, full of black heat. "Yes, of course I'll help out."

"You won't find yourself married to the wrong person," the dean said with a chuckle. "Although—" and Tessa wondered why he chose to look straight at her as he spoke "—I'm afraid there are many couples who discover too late that they've made the wrong choice."

Barbara Hannay was born in Sydney, Australia, educated in Brisbane and has spent most of her adult life living in tropical north Queensland, where she and her husband have raised four children. While she has enjoyed many happy times camping and canoeing in the bush, she also delights in an urban lifestyle—chamber music, contemporary dance, movies and dining out. An English teacher, she has always loved writing and now, by having her stories published, she is living her most cherished fantasy.

Books by Barbara Hannay

HARLEQUIN ROMANCE®
3578—OUTBACK WIFE AND MOTHER

Don't miss any of our special offers. Write to us at the following address for information on our newest releases.

Harlequin Reader Service
U.S.: 3010 Walden Ave., P.O. Box 1325, Buffalo, NY 14269
Canadian: P.O. Box 609, Fort Erie, Ont. L2A 5X3

THE WEDDING COUNTDOWN
Barbara Hannay

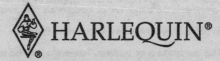

TORONTO • NEW YORK • LONDON
AMSTERDAM • PARIS • SYDNEY • HAMBURG
STOCKHOLM • ATHENS • TOKYO • MILAN • MADRID
PRAGUE • WARSAW • BUDAPEST • AUCKLAND

ISBN 0-373-03613-2

THE WEDDING COUNTDOWN

First North American Publication 2000.

Copyright © 1999 by Barbara Hannay.

This edition published by arrangement with Harlequin Books S.A.

Visit us at www.eHarlequin.com

Printed in U.S.A.

CHAPTER ONE

FOUR days to go...

'It's the most beautiful wedding dress ever!'

Tessa twirled in front of the long, oval mirror, her blue eyes shining as she watched her reflection. She turned and looked over her shoulder to examine the rear view of her elegant, low-backed gown. The exquisite detailing of the silk brocade bodice and the train of fine chiffon, drifting away from clusters of the palest of pale pink roses at her waist, combined to create a gown that was as pretty as a fairy tale.

'It's just perfect, darling,' Rosalind Morrow agreed, her gaze misty as she observed her daughter's happiness.

Flashing her mother an excited smile, Tessa paraded across the room, delighting in the luxurious rustle and whisper of expensive silk as she moved. 'It's going to be a dream wedding,' she sighed happily.

'Yes,' replied Rosalind, but her echoing sigh didn't sound quite so cheerful.

Tessa looked at her mother sharply. Rosalind's expression had grown cautious, and she twisted her hands nervously.

'Is something wrong, Mum?' Tessa asked.

'Of course not, darling, all the wedding plans are running like clockwork.' But then, in contradiction to her reassuring reply, Rosalind turned away. 'There's absolutely nothing wrong,' she went on with a shaky little laugh, 'but there is one tiny titbit of news.'

'Oh?' responded Tessa, suddenly tense, her heart thumping uncomfortably, 'What's that?'

Rosalind plucked at an invisible piece of lint on her neat navy linen skirt. 'You won't believe this,' she said, then paused and drew in a deep breath as if gathering courage to broach her news. 'Isaac's come home.'

Panic flashed through Tessa. She stared at her mother in silent horror. Her eyes flickered to her reflection in the mirror, and she saw the colour bleach from her face as Rosalind's words echoed crazily off her bedroom walls.

Isaac's come home. *Isaac's come home!*

From a long way off, she heard her mother's cry. 'Tessa, don't *look* like that!'

But then her ears filled with the deafening thud of her pounding heartbeat. The room, her mother and the reflection of her wedding gown blurred and swirled before her eyes. A sickening wave of dizziness swamped her.

'Tessa, for heaven's sake, you look terrible.'

Reaching behind her, Tessa felt for the edge of her bed, and when her hand touched the quilted cover, she sank gratefully onto it.

'Are you all right, dear?' Rosalind whispered, her mouth quivering into a frightened smile. 'Should I ring your father? How do you feel?'

Tessa struggled to gain composure. 'I'm fine. I—I forgot to eat any lunch today,' she said, lying, desperate to cover her panic. 'And...and you should have warned me about...about Isaac.'

'Of course I should,' Rosalind soothed. 'I guess I thought you were over him after all these years.'

'Over him, Mum? Of course I'm *over* him. I was never...' Tessa stopped abruptly. She quickly tried to change the subject. 'Help me up, please,' she said. She stood gingerly, trying to ignore the despair that threatened to engulf her.

Isaac's come home!

How could her whole world be up-ended so abruptly?

'Oh, dear. What will your father say? And your poor wedding dress! It *is* crushed.' Rosalind dithered as she checked her daughter's gown.

Mum, forget the dress! Tessa wanted to scream.

But, unaware of her daughter's consternation, Rosalind continued her inspection. 'At least there's no harm done that a steam iron can't fix,' she announced with relief as she finished at last. 'How are you feeling now, dear?'

Tessa tried very hard to smile, but the savage pounding in her chest would not subside, and the light-headedness threatened again. She had to stay on two feet!

'I'm fine, Mum,' she managed to reply without her voice cracking.

'At least you've already organised to come home to us for the rest of this week,' Rosalind added, eying her daughter with concern. 'You've been skipping lunch and now you're having...what was it? A dizzy spell? Clearly you're not looking after yourself properly, and I have enough to worry about. There's still so much to be done before Saturday.'

Tessa muttered something safely submissive while she tried to hide her mounting alarm. Being at home for the last few days before her wedding with her mother fretting and fussing over reception details was one thing, but if Isaac was home, as well!

That was impossible, unthinkable. What *was* Isaac doing home? Why now? Of all the disastrous luck! He'd stayed away for nine years. Surely he could have waited for a few more days. How could he do this to her?

If only she'd insisted on staying in her own flat until

Saturday, she thought with a stab of regret. But it was too late now. She'd already arranged for the new tenants to move in tomorrow.

Despair churned in Tessa's stomach. 'Would you mind making me a cup of peppermint tea, Mum? All the mugs and packets of tea and coffee are packed in a box on the kitchen bench.'

'Of course. That's just what you need. Let's get you out of this dress first. There's just one little rose to be reattached. Now, I'll undo the back and we'll have you out of there.' Rosalind prattled on as Tessa raised her arms and the dress was carefully lifted over her head. 'Don't worry, darling. By the end of the week you will be safely married to Paul, and then everything will be all right.'

Another wave of dizziness threatened Tessa.

'Everything will be fine then, won't it?' Rosalind asked.

'Of course,' Tessa answered softly.

As Rosalind made a beeline for the kitchen, her high heels tapping a no-nonsense beat across the terracotta tiles of the living area, Tessa mentally submerged that other question, the one that jumped out and startled her when she was least prepared. Sometimes it was there when she woke from restless dreams. Now it threatened her with renewed menace.

Of course she loved Paul!

She was really very happy. At least she was as happy as she could expect to be. She'd lost her chance for the Hollywood dream romance—that giddy once-in-a-lifetime kind of rapture—nine years earlier, when Isaac left. But there was absolutely nothing to be gained from dwelling on what happened to her when she was nineteen. She had a new life ahead of her now.

A good life.

And this unexpected return was not going to spoil it.

It had been a relief, after all the years of emptiness she'd suffered when Isaac left, to discover she was growing fond of Paul. He was so steady and obliging it was impossible not to find him charming. The fact that he had an enviable position in one of Townsville's top law firms and that his family and hers were old friends were added bonuses.

That was what she must focus on now.

Changed into casual clothes, Tessa appeared in the kitchen minutes later as her mother lifted the kettle and filled a mug with boiling water. 'Thanks,' she murmured, accepting the mug and gratefully sniffing the refreshing mint fragrance as she subsided onto a comfortable sofa.

Rosalind added milk to her cup of Earl Grey tea then sat down opposite her daughter, her long, slim legs crossed neatly.

'This is all very upsetting,' the older woman stammered. 'What a day I've had. First Isaac appearing out of the blue and now your little, er, spell. What would Paul think if he heard you were wobbly on your feet at the mere mention of another man's name?'

Tessa sighed and closed her eyes as she leant her head against the back of the sofa. She could feel the slanting rays of afternoon sunshine slipping through the wooden blinds and warming her closed eyelids. 'It wasn't just another man's name, Mum. There's quite a difference between hearing Isaac mentioned in passing and knowing that he's actually come home! After nine years, of course it's a shock. But,' she added, opening her eyes and forcing her voice to sound as flippant as she could manage, 'Isaac isn't really another man—not in the sense I think you're suggesting, anyhow. He's only my foster brother.'

'Oh, come on, Tessa,' Rosalind said sharply, stirring her tea with unnecessary vigour. 'I know you've always tried to hide your feelings for that foundling your father brought home, but...'

Tessa's mouth dropped open, and she stared wide-eyed at Rosalind. 'Mum, what are you talking about?'

Rosalind, her dark eyes fixed on her daughter's pale face, took an infuriatingly long sip of tea before she spoke. 'You don't really think your own mother didn't know what was going on, do you? My dear girl, from almost the day you turned fourteen, I watched you eat up that boy with your eyes whenever he was in the same room as you. All those hours you two spent away on the hill and down on the boat...'

The room swam. Tessa rubbed her eyes. She knew about the boat? How much did her mother know? Appalled, she took another sip of tea.

Rosalind continued. 'Then there was the dreadful mess you made of your science degree after Isaac went away.'

'But that was because...' *Because we were studying marine science together...going to save the world...planning to rescue every dolphin and discover the cure for cancer in some as yet undetected organism on the Great Barrier Reef.* '...because I was never much good at science anyway! And I was such a child then.'

Now, with an education degree behind her and a satisfying position as a preschool teacher, Tessa considered herself past this kind of parental interrogation and reprimand. An angry telltale pink crept up her neck, and she could feel it warming her cheeks.

'Of course it was a shock for all of us the way Isaac just disappeared without so much as goodbye,' Rosalind remarked. 'It nearly broke your father's heart, as you well know. After all those years of a good home, education, love, to just disappear without a trace. It was jolly ungrateful. And it's just too bad of him to come back now and spoil all our lovely plans.'

Tessa sat quiet and cold, listening to her mother's claims, unable to respond.

'But we mustn't let this spoil things, must we, dear?' Rosalind jumped up and took her cup and saucer to the kitchen. 'We must get going. You bring your gown and overnight bag. I'll look after these kitchen things. I think Paul has taken care of everything else, hasn't he?'

'Yes.'

'Let's get going, then.'

Home. To Isaac.

Under other circumstances, Tessa would have protested at her mother's domineering interference. Surely there was some alternative to living under the same roof as Isaac for the next four days? But the young couple who were to be the new tenants would never forgive her if she tried to change plans now. Places to rent were hard to find, and they had paid their bond and were so excited about having their own flat at last.

And in reality, given the hectic scattering and disordering of her thoughts since Isaac's name had first been mentioned, her ability to take any kind of control had completely dissolved.

It was all very well for Rosalind to claim that they mustn't let his return spoil things, but for Tessa, everything was totally spoiled already. The thought of Isaac home in Townsville sent her delicately rebuilt life teetering precariously, and she had absolutely no idea how much damage would result or how to avoid it.

She was terrified.

'I don't think you should drive for the rest of the week,' Rosalind said as she put her key to the lock of her smart, navy blue sedan. 'We can't have you fainting at the wheel.'

Tessa paused in the process of arranging her wedding dress on the back seat. 'I was nowhere near to fainting, Mum. Don't exaggerate. Now that I'm over the shock, I'll be fine. I—I've got Paul.' She slid into the passenger's seat next to her mother.

Rosalind paused before firing the ignition. 'Yes, you do have Paul, darling. Don't forget that. He's a dear man, and just right for you.' She steered the car into the late afternoon traffic.

A dear man, thought Tessa.

It was such an appropriate way to describe steady, dependable Paul. A dear man. A good man. No one had ever been tempted to describe Isaac that way. Sexy, sensuous, brooding, exciting, enticing, dangerous—the words that sprang to Tessa's mind to define Isaac flowed with alarming ease. And as she thought about him, a strange yearning, a shocking, unchecked wildness percolated fiercely along her veins. Hateful! She must always remember the truth about him, she reminded herself swiftly.

But she couldn't help asking, 'Where has Isaac been?'

Rosalind took a corner at a quite reckless speed. Then she replied, almost guiltily, 'To be honest, I've hardly spoken to him this afternoon. He did say something about mining over in Western Australia. Started out prospecting with some old fellow and worked his way up in the mining industry, I think. I believe he's been quite successful. But it's your father's afternoon off, and he just greeted Isaac with open arms like the returned prodigal son, opened his last bottle of his favourite vintage claret, and they've been chatting for hours. I'm afraid I was too distressed to just sit and listen to them. I have so much still to do, of course, and—well, you know how close they always were.'

The car pulled up with a slight screech as they encountered a line of traffic at an intersection.

Her father had always loved Isaac, Tessa reflected. Bringing the street kid home one night when he found him sick and shivering on the steps of his general practice surgery had been quite out of character for Dr. Morrow, but something in Isaac's intelligent, haunted face had touched the good man's heart long before the boy stole Tessa's. Isaac had lived with them for seven wonderful years after the official fostering papers had been signed.

And he'd been gone for nine after that fateful day.

Tessa quickly clamped down hard on her distracting thoughts and forced her mind to return to the safety of practical wedding plans. 'I can't wait to see the marquee when it's all decorated. Have the bud lights arrived?'

'Gardeners and Greene delivered all our orders this morning,' Rosalind replied.

'Great!' It was so easy to sound reassuringly interested in other things, but the attempts to keep her thoughts from straying to Isaac were unsuccessful. How could she bear to see him again now? Another alarming thought jumped into her head. 'Mum, Isaac's not going to stay for the— for my wedding, is he?'

The car was climbing through the streets of Yarrawonga, which, clinging to the edge of Castle Hill with stunning sea views, was Townsville's most prestigious suburb. They edged up the last steep incline to the Morrows' house.

'I have a strange feeling that might be why he came home,' said Rosalind, her voice brittle with tension. 'Of course, he claims he's here on business with some big

Asian mining company. But it is a strange coincidence, isn't it?'

Tessa's eyes stung with sudden hot tears. It was indeed very strange. And to have Isaac come back now, to have him present, actually watching her marriage to Paul Hammond, was worse than her most distressing nightmare. After all the long nights she'd lain in bed wondering about him, one minute crying for fear he was hurt or dead, and then wishing he was the next! How many times had her mind elaborated wildly on a bizarre range of horrific accidents?

Then eventually, after too long, she'd been numb enough to be able to force him to the back of her mind. And she had thrown herself into teaching her preschoolers with a passion that had delighted everyone and had brought her a measure of satisfaction. Her life, even if it felt continually at the low water mark, had resumed.

An off-the-road utility truck, black, new and very expensive looking, swathed in red dust, was parked in front of the Morrow house. It had to be Isaac's. The shock wave that jolted through Tessa hurt to her very fingertips.

She couldn't go inside, she decided. If seeing his car made her feel like this, how could she possibly face the man?

A blue heeler cattle dog sat in the back of the truck, keen eyes alert, ears pricked and tail wagging.

'Of course I've insisted the dog stays in the truck,' Rosalind muttered as she swung her car through the gates and swept up the steep drive beside the house. 'It would make a terrible mess of the garden.'

'Won't he—it—get hot?' asked Tessa lamely, wondering how any part of her mind could still function when she felt so dazed with dread.

'Isaac's brought a covered cage for him, and knowing

him, he'll take him for walks all over the hill. He'll be all right. July is our coolest month, after all,' replied Rosalind firmly as she wrenched on the handbrake and opened her door.

This was it.

Tessa tried to tell herself it was simply a matter of opening the car door, walking into her home and saying good afternoon to an old family friend. She would have preferred to walk into a creek full of man-eating crocodiles or into a dentist's surgery to have all her teeth drilled.

Trembling with tension, she followed her mother into the dimmed interior of the house, which was shuttered from the glare of the western sun. They stepped silently through the spotless kitchen and across the carpeted lounge towards the outside deck.

Isaac's voice, a familiar, deep, rumbling drawl, reached her first. Her heart thudded painfully. But what surprised her as she continued her journey was the sudden fatalistic calm that settled over her, as if the churning blood in her veins was transfused with something as soothing and innocuous as warmed honey.

It was almost as if she'd been sedated. She was able to dump her shoulder bag on the coffee table and walk towards the timber-framed doors that opened onto the deck as easily as she had when she was a thoughtless and carefree girl.

Is this how a fly feels as it enters a spider's web? she wondered. *Perhaps people heading for the guillotine experience this strange kind of peace in their final moments.*

All it took was the sound of Isaac's voice, and she was no longer fearful, but simply glad—overjoyed to be seeing her foster brother again.

And then her eyes found him.

Before she stepped out of the darkened room, she saw Isaac standing, looming against a railing at the end of the deck. She stayed in the shadows to steady the sudden fillip in her heartbeat. Sun-dappled light filtering through overhead lattice played across his features, highlighting first the aristocratic brow and then the craggy bone structure, which looked for all the world as if it had been sculpted by a passionately impatient hand. Except for the mouth, which was moulded firmly and carefully, with lips full of sensuous promise.

His hair was longer than she remembered. Curling and black, it skimmed his collar, so that more than ever he looked like a dark-skinned Gipsy or a pirate, wickedly adventurous, scorning convention. As he always had, Isaac carried that indefinable air of danger that should have repelled her, but had always drawn her to him—against her better judgment and to her intense regret.

Despite the obvious quality of his clothes, Isaac wore them with elegant negligence. The untidiness was rescued by his erect and handsome figure, the breadth of his shoulders, the leanness of his hips and the length of his legs.

It was totally unforgivable of her to immediately make comparisons, but it hit her at once that a man more different from Paul could hardly be found.

While Paul's face was round and placid, Isaac's was rugged and hard. Paul's eyes were a reflective, gentle grey. Isaac's were black fire smouldering beneath brooding, dark brows. Just now, his eyes were shaded, but she caught the glint of heated ebony.

Her impulse came in a heartbeat. She rushed forward, hurtling across the deck, a small missile flying into his startled arms.

'Isaac!'

After the countless hours she had idled away imagining

their meeting and Isaac's response, it was weird that now they were actually together again, her reaction was totally spontaneous, hopelessly unplanned.

And she gave herself no time to think of an aftermath. She simply buried herself into Isaac's chest and waited for his strong arms to close around her and to hold her tightly to him as they had so often before in happier times.

She felt the violent tremor that shuddered through his lean body as she pressed against it. But no arms descended to enclose her as she waited there. And when she cautiously looked into his face, she caught a momentary flash of agony swiftly replaced by a shield of cold indifference.

He stiffened, as if repelled by her advance, and the tiny, impoverished spark of faith she'd never quite extinguished through all the long years since he'd left was snuffed in an instant.

'Tessa, for heaven's sake.' Rosalind's choked disapproval clanged in the air behind her.

She drew back, her hands falling lifeless to her sides. 'Sorry,' she said softly. 'How...how are you, Isaac?'

'I'm fighting fit,' he replied, his eyes skittering ever so briefly over her hair, blond as ripe corn, her flushed face, simple blouse and slacks, then darting away to blink at the brick red bougainvillea, which hung from the trellis. 'And how are you, Tessa?'

'F-fine.'

'Let me congratulate you.' His eyes returned to her with lazy amusement, and he took her left hand, paying studious attention to her engagement ring. It was embarrassingly huge. An enormous emerald surrounded by brilliant diamonds. Tessa had always thought it too large and ostentatious for her fine bones, and because of her deep blue eyes, she hardly ever wore green, but Paul had been immensely proud of his selection.

As Isaac's dark gaze rested on the ring, her pale hand trembled visibly within the heat of his sun-tanned grasp.

'A fitting rock for the Queen of Castle Hill,' he said coldly.

Tessa snatched her hand away as if he'd burnt her. Reality with all its glaring, hateful commonsense showed her clearly what she had always known in her heart of hearts. Of course Isaac hadn't come back for her.

She had heard people throw away clichéd lines about moments of truth, but she had never realised what pain these moments represented.

If Isaac were oh so eager to see her again, he would never have stayed away so long in the first place. The accusations he'd flung at her the day he left were true. He despised her and everything she stood for. The very fact that he could come back now to watch coolly and dispassionately while she bound her heart and body to another man forever until parted by death meant that he felt no emotional ties whatsoever.

She knew it was ridiculous, but even as she stood there, angry at his easy rejection of her and still flushed with shame over her impetuous greeting, she was unable to drag her eyes away. They travelled restlessly, hungrily over his every feature while his gaze remained politely, icily remote.

At closer quarters, she sensed something about Isaac that was both as old and familiar as her memories of him and yet new and strange. It was as if he embodied a living contradiction. His dark, brooding eyes were shadowed by a weary sadness that suggested he'd been weighed down by too many harsh experiences. But beneath the stormy exterior there was something else, something sharp and expectant at his centre, something alert and waiting in his glittering gaze that made her think of the childish excitement of Christmas morning or the very first day of the long summer holidays.

She was startled when her father's voice broke into her thoughts. 'Tessa, darling, isn't this a wonderful surprise?'

She forced her lips to curve into a smile as she acknowledged her father's presence nearby in a comfortable squatter's chair. She crossed to him and bent to kiss his cheek. Like her fiancé, Paul Hammond, John Morrow was a kind and gentle man, if a little subservient to his wife. Tessa eyed her father fondly, remembering that it was Paul's likeness to him that had helped her decide to accept his proposal of marriage. A lifetime with someone like Dad would be very pleasant.

She wanted to concur with her father's pleasure in Isaac's return, but the words wouldn't form. Her mouth opened and then shut again. How could she possibly pretend to be pleased to see Isaac again? The wonderful surprise Dr. Morrow referred to had reverted to nightmare in the blink of a cold, indifferent eye.

But her father didn't seem to notice her hesitancy. 'Isaac's done so well!' He beamed at her. 'He's worked for a degree in mining engineering. He's slogged away for years out in the Pilbara. And now he manages a huge—'

'John,' interrupted Rosalind. 'Come and I'll make you a cup of tea. There's something I need to discuss with you.'

Tessa felt her mother's eyes linger on her a shade too long. She could imagine the detailed discussion of her dizzy spell. Poor Dad.

But sympathy for her father swiftly evaporated as the Morrows walked into the house, leaving Tessa and Isaac alone on the deck.

CHAPTER TWO

TESSA spun away from Isaac. How on earth could she face him alone? If only she could run after her parents like a frightened child! Her shaking hands gripped the deck's railing, and she forced her eyes to focus on the vista of rooftops and sea stretching below while she struggled to calm her rising panic. She took deep breaths, trying to think sensibly. Surely she'd faced the worst? Nothing could hurt her more than the monumental indifference of his cold greeting.

She flinched. How could she possibly have been so uncontrolled as to hurl herself at him like some immature groupie at a rock concert? Her ridiculous excitement at seeing Isaac had clearly embarrassed him. Of course he had stopped caring about her years ago.

'The view is as beautiful as ever.'

His voice brought her swivelling to face him. He was standing some distance away, but to her surprise, his eyes seemed to be exploring every inch of her face, as if they were taking in each fine detail, so that she could have been forgiven for thinking that the view he referred to was of herself. Self-consciously, she brushed a stray strand of hair from her face, and his eyes followed her hand—her left hand with its large emerald. And once more his face grew grim and hard.

A ridiculous urge to slip the ring from her finger seized Tessa, but of course that would be unthinkable for all sorts of reasons. But, with a momentary flash of guilt, she couldn't resist pushing her hand into the pocket of her slacks, hoping the gesture didn't look as contrived as it felt.

'I guess you've seen a great many places on your travels since you—you left,' she offered with a tight smile. 'How does this view compare with the rest of the world?'

Something resembling a smile flickered briefly at the corners of Isaac's mouth, revealing a glint of white teeth against his tan. His eyes, smouldering with secret amusement, travelled over her again, very slowly this time, then deliberately held her gaze. 'Oh, this view most surely holds its own,' he said softly.

Tessa felt a betraying heat flush her cheeks. Her throat tightened painfully, and goose bumps prickled her arms. Their sudden advent had nothing to do with the brisk sea breeze, which lifted and teased her hair. His gaze unleashed a rush of heady memories. Dangerous memories. This was unbearable! Think of Paul, she urged herself. Focus on the wedding.

'I—I still haven't travelled very far,' she said hoarsely, inching away from him.

Isaac nodded and smiled a little sadly as he looked out to sea. There was another awkward silence, and she wondered desperately what else they could talk about. 'I guess I should have taken the opportunity to travel widely by now,' she managed to say at last. 'Most of my friends have been overseas—to Asia, Europe, the States.'

'There's certainly a lot that can be learned from travelling,' Isaac replied, looking suddenly very serious, 'but then again, travel isn't always about distances covered— or sights seen.' His voice grew unexpectedly husky. He shoved his large hands deep into his trouser pockets and leant against the rail next to her. Tessa's gasp sounded as frantic as she felt. His voice, when he spoke again, was hardly more than a whisper. 'The important journeys can be going on inside us even when we appear to be standing still.'

He was looking at her as if his penetrating dark gaze could see right inside her heart. But Tessa knew he would never in a million light-years be able to trace all the miserable emotional journeys she had made in the past nine years—all of them going round and round in circles. Every one of them beginning and ending with her feelings for him.

I would have gone anywhere with you, Isaac, she wanted to cry.

Then, aghast at the insistence of her repeatedly disloyal thoughts, she moved away from the heat of his gaze, her mind boiling. To cover her consternation, she made a desperate stab at flippancy.

'You're getting very deep for so early in a conversation. Has your afternoon with Dad left you in a philosophical mood?'

Isaac's laugh sounded forced.

'Perhaps.' He took in a deep breath and stretched. His broad shoulders and chest expanded so that the loose cotton shirt lifted to reveal a tempting glimpse of smooth tanned flesh. Then he released his breath in a slumping sigh, and when Tessa lifted her gaze once more to his face, she wished she hadn't.

Isaac was looking at her as if she'd fulfilled his worst expectations.

'Of course,' he said, his lips twisted in a mirthless smile, 'I mustn't forget that when I'm with Queen Tess, deep is dangerous. We must stay comfortably shallow, mustn't we?'

Dismayed, she watched his face darken and his lips thin with bitterness until he looked as angry with her as he had on that horrible morning when he left. His sudden hostility baffled her now just as much as it had then.

On this very deck on a sultry November morning, over a breakfast neither of them had touched, he'd accused her of being shallow—of having all her middle-class values too firmly in place.

'Of course you're too fine a lady for a tramp who's crawled out of the gutter,' he'd stormed.

She shuddered as she remembered the accusations he'd hurled at her. In the midst of it all he'd called her a snob, and for the last time he'd labelled her Queen of Castle Hill. But it was the first time he'd made the name sound like an insult instead of a term of endearment.

She closed her eyes to stem the tide of burning tears that threatened. Now was certainly not the time to give in to the indulgence of hurtful indignation. 'I don't know about being shallow, but shouldn't we be aiming for less stress in our lives?' she asked lightly to cover her discomfort at the memories.

'Of course.' His shoulders moved in a scant shrug.

'You know the way it goes? Don't worry, be happy.'

'So you've been relaxed and happy?'

'As if you cared!' she snapped. 'You just walked off into the blue without giving me a second thought.'

Isaac's eyes narrowed. His mouth thinned into another unhappy smile, and he shook his head.

'You can't deny it!' she cried, her eyes bright with anger. Then before her courage drained away, she spoke the question uppermost in her mind. 'Why have you come back, Isaac?'

But she didn't get the answer she so desperately needed. The sudden loud, aggressive barking of a dog interrupted them. It was coming from somewhere on the footpath.

'That sounds like Devil.' Isaac strode quickly to the far end of the deck and, driven by curiosity, Tessa followed. By leaning over the deck's railing, they could look down, past the side of the house, to the front footpath.

Isaac's dog was straining at his leash, snarling and barking madly and trying desperately to leap over the edge of the utility. It seemed he wanted to attack someone on the footpath.

'Devil, stop that! Down, boy!' he called.

Devil! What an appropriate name for a hateful man's dog, Tessa thought. Then she looked more closely at the cowering victim on the footpath.

'Oh, good heavens. It's Paul. Your dog's after my fiancé,' she cried.

Paul Hammond stood on the footpath, trying manfully to ignore the dog's fury. At Isaac's instruction, Devil stopped barking, but he still growled, his lip curled and his teeth bared.

'Don't touch Devil, he's a one man dog,' barked Isaac in a fierce imitation of the snarling animal.

'I've no intention of touching him,' Paul called. 'I simply spoke to him.'

'He's trained to be a good watchdog,' Isaac muttered, glaring at Paul with something close to malice.

Tessa felt compelled to defend her fiancé. 'Come on up, Paul,' she said. She turned to Isaac. 'I hope your dog won't attack all our visitors. Poor Paul—what an awful introduction for him.'

'*Poor* Paul,' repeated Isaac softly, 'should know better than to approach strange dogs.'

Paul's footsteps could be heard at the bottom of the stone steps leading from the side garden onto the deck.

'I do hope you'll be civilised and pleasant,' muttered Tessa swiftly. 'You remember Paul Hammond, of course.

He lives in the split-level house on the corner, and he was a few years ahead of us at school.'

'Oh, yes. I remember him,' replied Isaac with a sickly smile. 'He played the tuba in the school band, didn't he? Is he still tubby?'

'No. He certainly is not!' retorted Tessa as her fiancé, looking only slightly flushed, reached the top of the steps and waved a greeting to them.

'Darling,' cried Tessa, running towards him. 'I'm sorry about the rude reception. Just as well that brute was chained up.'

'Oh, don't worry about it.' Paul smiled bravely before kissing Tessa neatly on the cheek. 'For some reason the mutt just didn't fancy me. He started growling when I was still metres away.'

Tessa suppressed any disloyal thoughts about animals and their reputed ability to judge character. 'He's obviously very badly trained,' she retorted, glaring at Isaac and slipping her arm through Paul's.

Paul looked pleased and patted her hand. 'Oh, I don't know,' he began gallantly, but Tessa hurried on.

'Let me introduce you to Isaac. You remember my foster brother.'

'Isaac Masters? Good heavens! Is that who your visitor is? I couldn't see from the footpath without my glasses.'

'Been a long time,' said Isaac, nodding curtly and stretching his hand in greeting.

'He's turned up unexpectedly,' said Tessa, wishing that there were not so many factors she had to ignore all of a sudden. Paul's hand looked so very pale and slight as Isaac's tanned fingers grasped it in a strong grip, and his answering smile looked more like a grimace. But what bothered her especially was that Isaac seemed so relaxed

and in control, when she felt as if her entire body was
being pushed through a paper shredder.

She hated Isaac for looking so cool and unconcerned—
for not caring that the girl he once promised to love forever was about to be married to someone else.

'How are you, Paul?' Isaac asked politely.

'Never better, Zac,' responded Paul rather loudly. He
shot an arm around Tessa's shoulders and drew her to
him. 'And what do you think of our news, Zac? Tessa's
about to make me the luckiest man in North Queensland.'

A small muscle twitched in Isaac's cheek, and his eyes
seemed to be mesmerised by Paul's thumb as it stroked
Tessa's shoulder.

'Well, Tub—sorry, Paul—I'd say you could probably
stretch that territory at least as far as the whole east coast
of Australia. I've been congratulating Tessa already and
admiring her superb engagement ring. It's quite a spectacular rock. I wish you both all the very best, and I'm
looking forward to being part of the nuptial celebrations.'

'You're staying for the wedding?' The question sprang
from Tessa's lips like the cry of a startled cockatoo.

'Of course,' replied Isaac smoothly. 'I couldn't miss out
on the big day. Hell, Tess, I'm family. You wouldn't turn
me away, would you?'

Of course I would, her mind screamed.

'Certainly not,' answered Paul heartily. 'The more the
merrier. Everyone who's anyone in Townsville will be
there. I'm sure Rosalind's already included you on our
guest list.' He added this as his future mother-in-law
stepped onto the deck.

'Paul, how lovely.' Rosalind smiled a warm greeting.
Her eyes frosted a little as they moved to Isaac. 'Did I
overhear you saying you intend to come to the wedding,
Isaac?'

'Yes,' Paul cut in eagerly before Isaac could reply. 'That'll be fine, won't it, Ros?'

Out of the corner of her eye, Tessa glimpsed the upward movement of Isaac's eyebrow. Ros? Zac? She'd never heard Paul shorten either Rosalind's or Isaac's names before. No one ever did. She wondered if Paul was dredging up bonhomie to cover a sudden rush of insecurity. But surely he didn't know anything that could make him feel threatened by Isaac?

'Isaac must come if he'd like to,' Rosalind replied carefully.

'Thank you,' said Isaac. 'I would certainly be honoured to attend Townsville's wedding of the year.'

'Wedding of the year? Oh, I don't know about that, but we're trying hard.' Rosalind laughed. 'We just have to keep both Tessa's feet on the ground for the rest of the week.'

'Getting light-headed with excitement?' queried Isaac, eyeing Tessa darkly.

As she met his penetrating glance, Tessa felt her heart jolt so savagely she feared another wave of dizziness.

'Take good care of our little girl over the next few days, Paul,' said Rosalind pointedly. 'She almost fainted this afternoon.'

'Good heavens!' Paul squinted at Tessa, examining her closely. 'Are you feeling better now, dear?' he asked.

'I'm perfectly fine,' Tessa responded quickly. 'I just got a nasty shock, that's all. Nothing at all for you to worry about, Paul. Dad's keeping a close professional eye on me.'

But Isaac was staring at her with a strange expression, and she quickly turned her back on him. Despite the fresh evening air sweeping in from the Coral Sea, she felt dreadfully claustrophobic.

'Can I help with dinner, Mum?' she asked. 'Paul, you'll eat with us, won't you?' Before he could reply, she rushed on. 'I'll leave you folk to get reacquainted. You know how to help yourselves to the bar, don't you? I'm sure Dad will join you in a moment.'

She knew her rapid withdrawal was cowardly, but suddenly there were too many people, too many issues. If she was to avoid making a complete fool of herself, she had to get away.

She stumbled into the kitchen and slumped against a bench. 'I can't do this!' she cried aloud. 'I'm going to go mad before this week's out.' Her fist slammed onto the bench so fiercely it hurt, but she hardly noticed. The rest of her was already hurting, smarting, bruised.

She took a long, deep breath and then another. There was only one way to cope with this dreadful situation, she decided. She had to keep busily focused on little tasks. After all, when she really thought about it, every day was made up of a string of little tasks. It should be straightforward. Her mission was to get through the next four days. If she gave each separate task her devoted attention, she would find herself at the end of the week in no time at all, and this whole ordeal with Isaac would be over.

She'd be married.

Feeling slightly stronger, Tessa set about the first task, preparing the Thai chicken stir fry that she and her mother had planned. She dragged Rosalind's huge wok out of the cupboard and began to assemble the ingredients. Chicken strips, capsicum, carrots, snow peas. There was a bottle of sweet chilli sauce in the fridge. Excellent. And some fresh coriander…

She flicked the switch on the transistor radio, and the strains of Ella Fitzgerald crooning 'Summertime' filled the room. That was better. The lush swell of the music began to calm her. Tessa kicked off her shoes and padded about the kitchen in her bare feet as she found a chopping board and a suitable knife. Then she began to slice the carrots.

'Need a hand?'

Tessa swung round, and her sudden movement sent a carrot rolling off the bench. Isaac was standing mere inches behind her.

'Whoa!' He ducked and neatly caught the vegetable centimetres from the floor.

'What are you doing here?' she snapped, her heart wildly thumping again.

'Rescuing falling carrots.' He grinned. 'And clearly not enjoying the warmth of your welcome.'

'I'm glad you've got the message.'

'That I'm not welcome?'

'Exactly. I came in here to get some peace.'

'But this is a big job, Tess.' Isaac surveyed the assembled collection of vegetables. 'You'll be chopping here for ages. You need another pair of hands.'

'Mum will be in soon.'

'I don't think so. She's on the phone to some relative of Paul's having an in-depth conversation about seating arrangements at the reception. Things were getting a touch heated.'

Isaac sauntered across the room and picked up another chopping board before selecting a sharp knife.

'Give me a job, Tessa.'

She glared at him. 'If you insist, I'll need some onions sliced. You can do that. You'll find them in the bottom of the pantry.' It would serve him right if the onions made his eyes water, she thought triumphantly as she turned once more to her carrots. Why couldn't Isaac leave her alone? She offered him her back as she chopped slowly and carefully, angling the knife to produce slim oval slices.

'Summertime' finished on the radio, and Ella Fitzgerald began another number. The instant Tessa heard the opening bars of 'I'm In the Mood for Love,' her hand shot out to snap the radio off. And in the echoing silence, she heard Isaac's knife drumming rhythmically against the wooden board. She turned. Isaac was slicing onions with the speed and dexterity of a professional chef. 'Isaac! Where on earth did you learn to chop onions like that?'

He looked up, feigning innocence. 'Like what?'

Tessa rolled her eyes. 'I thought it was mining engineering you've been studying, not cooking.'

Isaac slid the pile of finely sliced onions into a bowl and picked up a capsicum. He tossed it lightly then held it out as if studying the smooth, bright red skin. 'I've discovered all sorts of hidden talents in the last nine years, Tess.'

Tessa's eyes closed automatically as a wave of painful jealousy washed over her. Jealousy for all those years in Isaac's life she hadn't shared. What had he been doing? And who had shared all these hidden talents?

Why should she care?

'I dare say you've learned a great deal, too,' he added and shot her a searching glance. Then his face relaxed into a mocking grin as his gaze rested on her small pile of carrots. 'But perhaps not in the kitchen.'

'You grub!' Tessa yelled. 'You've barged in here when you're not wanted. You've taken over the place, and now you're making snide remarks about my ability in the kitchen! It's a pity you didn't learn some modesty along with all your multi-skilling.'

Isaac ducked as Tessa let fly with the last of her carrots just as Rosalind walked into the kitchen.

'What's going on in here?' she demanded.

'I'm making a nuisance of myself,' said Isaac with a grin. 'So I'll leave you two in peace.' He retrieved the carrot from its landing place in the sink and placed it carefully on the bench in front of Tessa. Then he winked at her before walking quietly out of the room.

Of course she couldn't sleep.

All evening endless questions and haunting memories distracted and tormented her, but once she was in bed, alone in her room, they marched through Tessa's mind with relentless lucidity. What on earth had possessed Isaac to come back now? What was the real reason for his return? Had he heard about the wedding? Surely, as Rosalind had said, it was too much of a coincidence that his business would bring him to Townsville on this particular week.

He was more self-contained, more confident now than he had been when she knew him before. That had probably come with success. Success in business and in love, most likely.

Tessa flopped onto her stomach and tried to blank out the tormenting thoughts. Just breathe deeply and relax, she told herself. She lay in the dark trying hard to empty her mind. But soon the taunting images came rolling back. She thought of Isaac lying down the hall. Was he snoring blissfully, or was he remembering, too? How had he felt today when he drove up to the house?

For seven years it had been his home.

She pictured him sitting in his truck staring at the house for several moments before he began to climb the curve of smooth sandstone steps bordered by drifts of bright bougainvillea. In her mind's eye she saw his long legs taking the steps two at a time. Did he encounter, as she so often did when she came home, the ghosts of a laughing, golden-haired girl and a tall, dark, brooding boy?

And when he stepped out onto the deck and saw once again the blue sweep of Cleveland Bay and the mass of tall, straight masts, which delineated the marina, did he remember *Antares?* She felt her cheeks grow hot. What a fiery couple they had been when she was nineteen and he one year older. Alone on the family yacht, they'd seduced each other with all the excitement and passion of intense, young love.

How special that time had been!

She could still remember the delicious smell of Isaac's sun-warmed skin as she buried her face in his chest, the taste of his lips on hers and the reassurance of his arms holding her tight. And especially she remembered the way he'd looked at her, his dark eyes smouldering with desire, and how her senses exploded with longing.

Paul Hammond's serious face flashed into Tessa's mind, and she knew at once that she had to stop thinking about Isaac. Sleep was going to be impossible. She wondered if Rosalind kept any chamomile tea.

Putting her thoughts into action, Tessa padded down the dark, silent hallway to the kitchen. Luckily Rosalind's big pantry cupboard was fixed with an internal light, so she could find the herbal tea bags without having to illuminate the whole area. She left the pantry door open and used the glow from its light while she found a mug and boiled the kettle.

She placed two tea bags in a small teapot, filled it, then carried it and a mug onto the moon-washed deck. It was cool outside, and she was glad of her warm pyjamas as she settled into a canvas director's chair, hoping the silvery bay and the distant lights of Magnetic Island would soothe her.

'I'll have whatever you're having.'

'Oh, Lord!'

Isaac was sitting in the shadows a few feet away. He was grinning at her. 'I'll just duck inside and get myself a mug,' he said calmly, while Tessa's heart pounded more painfully than ever.

This was getting ridiculous! Wasn't there anywhere in her parents' home where she could have some privacy?

When Isaac returned with a mug, Tessa tried to overlook the vast amount of male body outlined by his black silk boxer shorts and skimpy black T-shirt. 'So you drink chamomile tea?' she asked, but how could she think about herbal tea when he was so disturbingly beautiful? Apart from the hidden talents he'd alluded to earlier, Isaac had developed some rather spectacular physical attributes. He must have spent a great deal of the last nine years working his body hard, because his chest and arms were more deeply muscled than ever. And life in the outdoors had tanned his naturally dark complexion. She had to force her eyes away from feasting on him.

'Chamomile?' Isaac's eyebrow arched, and then he grinned. 'I'll try anything once.'

Tessa kept her eyes steadily on the task of pouring his tea. 'I find it helps me to sleep,' she said as she filled the mugs. 'I'm into herbal teas these days. I keep quite a range.'

'Surely there are better ways to make you sleepy, Tess,' Isaac murmured as he drew a chair next to hers and sat down.

Feeling her cheeks start an annoying blush, Tessa retorted, 'Aren't you cold? It's the middle of winter, you know.'

Isaac chuckled. 'People who live in the tropics don't know what winter is.' His amused eyes took in her sensible pink flannelette pyjamas buttoned to the neck, with long sleeves and long legged pants. 'Don't tell me you're taking those on your honeymoon.'

She glanced at him sharply. In the moonlight his dark eyes teased her.

'Of course not,' she answered swiftly, but the startling image of Isaac viewing her in the elegant lace and silk affair she'd bought for her honeymoon crept traitorously into her mind and sent her cheeks flaming again. Her heart shot around in her rib cage at maniacal speed.

'I see you haven't lost that habit,' Isaac observed, interrupting her dangerous thoughts.

'Habit?' Tessa asked wildly.

He reached for her hand as it twisted a lock of hair.

'You still fiddle with your hair when something's bothering you,' he said softly. She snatched her hand from the side of her head. But she was mesmerised by his proximity and by the way he stared at the strand of hair she had loosened, bright yellow against his dark skin. He rolled the lock between supple fingers and thumb.

'Spun gold,' he whispered. 'Remember how I threatened to cut off a lock of your hair if you kept twisting it?'

'You did cut it off,' Tessa whispered back. 'When I was sixteen. And it took ages to grow back.'

'So I did.' His face was only inches from hers. He stared again at the lock of hair in his hand, then frowned and dropped it abruptly.

'I—I think I'll take my drink to the bedroom,' she said, stammering. It was going to take more than chamomile tea to help her relax.

'Speaking of bedrooms,' Isaac replied quickly, before she could stand up.

'Which we weren't,' Tessa retorted, but Isaac continued as if he hadn't noticed.

'I was very surprised to find my old room just as it's always been. I was certain Rosalind would have totally redecorated it by now.'

Tessa shrugged, wondering if Isaac could guess that she had begged her mother to leave everything untouched. She had known it was illogical, but she'd clung to the superstitious hope that, by changing nothing in his room, she could somehow keep Isaac's feelings for her intact, as well.

And so the room had stayed the same. The oak desk remained by the window, and lined along the windowsill were fossilised sea creatures embedded in ancient rock. Even Isaac's dried-out starfish and sea-urchin collections had been retained, although now the ancient white skeletons were tastefully arranged in cane decorator baskets.

'All those marine creatures,' she said, twisting the mug in her hands. 'I don't suppose they have much relevance in your life any more.'

'Not really,' he replied, taking a sip of tea and pulling a wry face. He seemed about to comment on the brew, then shrugged. 'I've virtually turned my back on the sea and diverted my focus to the land—to the very bowels of the earth, I suppose you could say.'

'And you like it over in Western Australia?'

He let out a brief sigh. 'I've been successful there,' he replied evasively, then added, 'if monetary gain counts as success.' He stared at the contents of his mug. 'Parts of that state are superb. The Kimberley region fascinates me. It has to be among the best wilderness areas in the world. But the mines of Western Australia are completely different from the North Queensland coast. But, you see, being there made forgetting easier.'

Tessa slumped low in her seat. The mug almost slipped from her limp grasp. 'Forgetting?' she managed to whisper, although her throat swelled painfully. 'You wanted to forget everything here?'

'It makes sense not to cling to unpleasant memories, doesn't it?'

Unpleasant memories! How could he say that? She had fretted and pined and made herself sick over someone who'd been doing his damnedest to get her out of his mind.

Tessa sat up straight and lifted her chin even as hot tears sprang in her eyes. 'It makes perfect sense,' she told him. 'I've certainly put the past behind me.'

'Where it belongs,' he said softly, his face grim. 'You've done well, Tessa. You've built a new career, acquired a husband-to-be, and all those fine and fancy wedding presents are piling up.'

How could he make the simple truth sound so insulting? Tessa knew if she stayed another minute, the telltale tears would fall.

She jumped to her feet. 'When you go away again,' she said as airily as she could, 'you should make sure you take that old lamp you made from the bailer shell with you,' and then she quickly hurried across the deck and into the house before he could reply.

CHAPTER THREE

THREE days to go...

In the early hours, Tessa eventually fell into a deep, troubled sleep and didn't wake until footsteps in the corridor outside her room stirred her. She woke up slowly and then—slam—she remembered the previous night. And Isaac. She groaned and pulled the pillow over her head.

She didn't want to face the day.

But, she consoled herself, it was already Wednesday, and there were only three days left till her wedding day. Closing her eyes, she was suddenly grateful for all her mother's big plans. With so many details to attend to she shouldn't need to see much of Isaac. Tomorrow the preschool would close for the end of semester holiday, and in the evening a rehearsal of the ceremony had been arranged for the wedding party. Friday would no doubt be spent frantically supervising last-minute preparations. And Saturday was her wedding day.

Tessa hugged the pillow tightly to her chest. She only had to survive for a little longer. Then she would be married to Paul and she could put Isaac out of her mind. Forever.

There was a tap on her door. It opened gently, and her father stepped into the room. 'I'm off to do some hospital rounds before surgery starts. Just brought you a cuppa.'

'Oh, Dad, how lovely. Thank you.'

John Morrow placed the cup and saucer carefully on

her bedside table. 'How are you feeling this morning, possum?'

'Fine,' she lied.

'You needed a good night's sleep.' Her father leant down and kissed Tessa's cheek. Then he straightened and looked at her thoughtfully. His eyes, the clear blue that she'd inherited, were narrowed slightly behind his spectacles.

Tessa returned his gaze but could think of nothing to say. Her father loved Isaac, too. He was delighted to have him back—but for him there were no complications.

As if he guessed the direction of her thoughts, Dr. Morrow spoke. 'Isaac's been up for hours, roaming with that dog of his on the hill, I think. I've told your mother to let him know he's welcome to go sailing if he wants to. There's a good south-easterly forecast for today, and *Antares* needs a run.'

Tessa nodded. 'He'd like that, I'm sure.' She was relieved when her father left after giving her hair a quick ruffle. She reminded herself once more of her task for the next three days—to simply survive and to get herself safely married to Paul Hammond.

But there was nothing simple about survival, she realised as, after showering and dressing for work, she discovered Isaac, dressed in a skimpy athletics singlet and shorts, tucking into a huge bowl of tropical fruit and muesli at the breakfast table. Her appetite dwindled at the sight of him sitting there as if he belonged, just as he had through all her teenage years.

It was dangerously like the morning she'd first realised she was in love with him.

It had happened at breakfast one morning when she'd looked up sleepily from her cereal and toast. He'd grinned at her, and then unexpectedly his dark eyes had flared with black heat as they slid to the pale skin of her shoulder and the tops of her ripening breasts, inadvertently exposed when her thin cotton nightdress slipped sideways.

And in a heartbeat, she'd responded to that look, her senses leaping to an entirely new level of awareness. With a sudden clarity of vision, she had understood the secret messages his eyes signalled. And just as suddenly, Tessa realised that this young person she lived with was a magnificent specimen of masculinity. How was it that until then she had never really appreciated the breadth of his shoulders, the sculpted muscles, the strength in his brown hands and the sweet, secretive depths of his eyes?

It was if she'd entered another level of existence. And it was shortly after that morning that Rosalind insisted she must no longer stumble out to breakfast in her nightdress.

'I'd forgotten the taste of a perfect tropical pawpaw,' Isaac commented as she edged shakily into a seat at the far side of the table.

'They've been superb lately,' Tessa muttered, her stomach quaking all over again at his early morning appearance. There was no doubt about it, her impression last night had been quite correct. He was a downright male miracle.

'What time do you usually leave for work?' he asked.

'Oh, er, eight o'clock,' she stammered.

'Then you'd better eat up. It's almost that now.'

'I don't think I can face breakfast this morning. I'll just have a coffee,' she said, reaching for the pot.

'Tess, you know that's very foolish. No wonder people are worried you'll keel over at the drop of a hat. Here, at least have half my toast.' He took a slice of wholemeal toast, spread it with marmalade, cut half for himself and held the other half out to her. And he smiled a warm smile that mesmerised her with bewildering ease. 'That's better,' he said as she bit into the crust, her eyes still held by his. Then, flipping a set of car keys onto the table, he told her, 'I'm to be your chauffeur, so let me know when you're ready.'

The absurd spell was broken. 'My chauffeur?' She shook her head. 'But that's ridiculous. I'm perfectly capable of driving myself. It's totally unnecessary!'

'I'm afraid it is quite necessary. Rosalind's busy, John's already left, and you're not to drive because of your, er, condition. I'm afraid I'm your only hope.'

'My condition? What nonsense.'

'I guess it must be a pain in the neck to be ordered not to drive, but that's your father's strict instruction. I've heard it from both him and from Rosalind.' He was smiling as he looked at her, his eyes alight and teasing, but the next minute, Tessa wondered if it were bravado. Quite suddenly Isaac frowned, and his relaxed manner evaporated while his eyes darkened and his face grew taut. 'Tess,' he began, and then paused, his throat working as he clenched and unclenched his fists. 'You're not pregnant, are you?'

'For heaven's sake, Isaac!' Tessa's cheeks flared. 'What on earth makes you ask that?'

'It's just that everyone's treating you like you're so damned delicate.'

'Of course I'm not pregnant. That's impossi—' She bit her tongue so hard it hurt. There was no way she wanted Isaac to know the intimate secrets of her demure relationship with Paul. Of course, there was nothing wrong with their love life. Surely it was possible for a successful marriage to grow from a relationship that started with limited physical desire. All that came later...when necessary. But she wouldn't expect Isaac to understand such things. He was an animal when it came to passion. She could never imagine behaving with Paul as she had with Isaac.

And that was just as well! What she needed was a calm, sedate life. She'd had enough turmoil to last her the rest of her days.

But it wasn't going to get any better just yet.

Isaac was regarding her with a searching stare, his heavy brows drawn low over dark glittering eyes, and a shaft of something like electricity chased around her stomach. He picked up the keys and jingled them in one hand.

'When you're ready, m'lady.'

'This is hopeless,' she said, fuming. 'The last person I want to be driving around with all week is *you!*'

His fist snapped tightly around the keys as his eyes narrowed to black cracks in his hard face. 'You surprise me, Queen Tess. I thought you'd be pleased to see me put in my place—as your servant.'

There it was again. This snide implication that she was a first-class snob. What had she ever done to make him hate her so fiercely? His contempt for her was obvious in the curl of his lip and the thrust of his jaw. She spun away, blinking back tears, and went to collect her things.

In the seconds before she flounced off, however, her eyes caught a bleak shadow of sadness flickering across his face before it was swiftly replaced by a mocking grimace. When she returned with a bulging carryall ready for work, Isaac's expression had settled into hard-edged anger. He looked as if he would like to grab her and shake her. Tessa frowned. Why was he so angry? She couldn't believe he was bothered about the kind of relationship she had with the man she planned to marry.

It wasn't as if he wanted her for himself.

She pinned her lips into a tight smile. 'I'm ready, Jeeves.'

He offered her a mock bow, and she knew he was trying to annoy her. The motion conveyed no trace of hu-
mility, but he lifted the carryall from her shoulder with
athletic grace. She followed him down the short flight of
steps to the garage.

'Do we have far to drive?' he asked.

'Not really—only to South Townsville.' She stopped
on the second last step, causing him to turn. 'Isaac…' He
stared at her speculatively. 'About staying here till the
wedding,' she said nervously. 'You don't have to, you
know. I mean, you've been gone for so long. Why come
back now?'

'It really bothers you?'

She reached for the iron rail beside her. 'No, of course
it doesn't *bother* me. But you don't like Paul particularly…'

'What makes you say that?'

Her shoulder lifted in a tiny shrug. 'I guess it's just
something I've sensed.'

Isaac stood very still staring at her. His gaze seemed to
read the very depths of her soul. He was silent for the
longest time, and Tessa kept a strong grip on the railing.

'Then you've sensed wrongly,' he replied at last, speaking so softly she could only just hear the words. His voice
rose. 'But I'll be damned if I'm going to start praising the
fellow just to make you feel better.'

'Of course, I don't need you to—'

'Besides, it doesn't really matter how I feel about your
man, does it? I'm not marrying him.'

'No, I didn't mean—' Tessa shook her head desperately.

Isaac swung her bag casually over his shoulder and
turned towards the car. 'You love him, and that's all that
counts. Isn't that right?'

'Y-yes. Of course.'

'So if it doesn't bother you to have me here, and the sight of your bridegroom doesn't worry me in the slightest, is there really a problem?'

Tessa shook her head dazedly and stepped towards the car. 'No problem. Let's go,' she muttered and walked quickly to the passenger door, waiting for him to unlock it for her.

They drove through the city in silence, but as they approached South Townsville, Isaac looked at the railway yards and old sheds curiously.

'I'm surprised you're not working in one of the *newer* suburbs,' he commented. 'But I suppose gentrification of inner suburbs has reached Townsville as well as the southern cities.'

'To a certain extent,' Tessa agreed. 'Trendy couples are buying old Queenslander cottages and renovating and extending them to look just like the pictures you see in house and garden magazines.'

'And I guess it's the offspring of these young and upwardly mobile professionals who attend your admirable preschool,' he said, shooting her a knowing glance.

'So what are you implying?' she asked. She had a fair idea. He considered her a snob at work as well as in her private life.

'Don't fret, Tessa. I'm sure you give these smart young fry a flying start in the education rat-race.' A brief smile illuminated his face.

But the smile evaporated with her next words. 'My school is over here on the left.'

Isaac applied the brake and changed gears while trying to locate the spot Tessa indicated. He stared at the dilapidated, long, low building of fibro painted a garish yellow trimmed with red, then blinked as he focused on a sign

painted near the front entrance—Burrawang Day Care and
PreSchool Centre.

'This is it?' he asked, as he pulled into the kerb, unable
to disguise the surprise in his voice.

'Yes,' she replied with a smile, enjoying his shock and
already looking forward to the day ahead. She loved her
work. 'Thanks for the lift, Isaac.'

As she opened her door, his hand on her arm stilled
her. 'How about I pick you up and we catch a bite to eat
at lunchtime?'

Tessa's smile froze. 'Oh, I can't possibly get away then.
I have to supervise the children's lunches.'

'Don't you have any assistants?'

'Yes, two wonderful women, but...'

'I'm sure they'd let you off for half an hour or so. I
think we need to talk—to set things straight before the
big day.'

'I—I don't know,' Tessa demurred. She needed a day
free from Isaac—a chance to catch her breath, to refocus
on her wedding. 'Aren't you going sailing? Dad said you
should take *Antares* for a run.'

'I think it would be wise if we talk things through,' he
said. 'I might go for a sail late this afternoon. But we
need to lay a few ghosts before you embark on your new
life.'

'Do you really think so?' she muttered.

'Damn sure of it.'

'Won't it mean going over *unpleasant* memories?'

Isaac stared at her, and the hand on the steering wheel
clenched. For a moment she wondered if he regretted the
impulsive invitation. 'Let's hope not,' he said, shifting his
gaze to the road ahead. 'I'm sure we can manage a civilised, adult conversation.'

'All right then,' she replied uncertainly. 'Pick me up at one o'clock.'

She told herself she could do it. She would steer away from dangerously provocative topics—like his reasons for abandoning her. He'd take her to lunch and tell her all about his success in his business. And she would tell him about Paul's plans to build a house on the hill. After they'd both been through the superficial exercise of fulfilling each other's expectations, she would feel better. She'd be able to waltz past him down the aisle on Saturday and she wouldn't feel a thing.

That was the plan.

At one o'clock she met him just inside the door. She was almost getting used to the impact of his spellbinding male elegance, even in jeans and a white polo shirt.

'I'd like to come in and have a squiz around if I may,' he surprised her by asking.

Frowning, Tessa stepped back and gestured for him to continue inside.

'I've never been in one of these places. Never went to one myself, of course,' he said with a self-conscious laugh. 'My mother was always too...'

'Of course, Isaac,' Tessa murmured soothingly. He looked as if his confidence had suddenly deserted him, and Tessa's heart leapt. 'Many of these children have mothers like yours....'

She didn't continue. There was no point in filling in the details about his deserted mother, who'd clung to her drug addiction as an excuse to never recover after his father left them and was later reported killed. He'd shared the horrors of his early childhood with her once, in the days when she thought he trusted her.

'You can have a look around if you like,' she replied. 'It's all pretty simple.'

He rubbed his chin thoughtfully as his eyes took in the building, little more than a galvanised iron shed, no better inside than out. 'I had a vague idea that preschools were modern airy buildings with large tinted windows and set in landscaped gardens with plenty of shade cover and elaborate play sculptures.'

'Most are,' Tessa admitted. 'I'm afraid this is a poor charity affair.'

She watched him wander around, pausing before the old pine kitchen table that served as her desk and at the other ancient tables with plastic-coated tops, their legs sawn down to a preschooler's height. They were lined down the middle of the floor space. On each table was a cluster of plastic containers that had once held takeaway meals but now were filled with crayons, coloured paper, pipe-cleaners or pieces of foil. The floor was bare concrete, swept clean. And there was a touch of luxury—a square of faded carpet and a pile of tattered beanbags in one corner.

But if the primitive structure and resources surprised him, the sight of the children who played there seemed to deliver a low blow to Isaac's gut. He stared at them, his face suddenly pale beneath its tan. 'These children...they're underprivileged?'

'What did you expect?' she asked. 'Clean, well dressed, well fed youngsters with shining hair and confident faces?'

'I—I guess so.'

In stark contrast to the thin but happy children, who ran to a low water trough to wash their hands for lunch, Isaac looked thoroughly miserable. He stared at the children's undernourished bodies and their threadbare or ill-fitting clothes.

'And you choose to work here?'

'Yes, I do,' said Tessa with a shrug of her slim shoulders. 'I know it's very basic. We have no money to speak of. All their parents are unemployed. But we have fun.'

She moved across the room to help a small boy with thick spectacles and thin arms turn off a tap. Isaac watched them, his eyes black and disconsolate. He rubbed his hands across his face as if somehow he could erase the picture before him.

'If it's any consolation, Paul doesn't like my working here, either,' she said as she joined him again. 'In fact he hates it.'

'Oh, it—it's not that I object to it,' Isaac began.

'But you weren't ready to have your image of me as a comfortable, pampered princess swept away so swiftly?'

He shrugged uncomfortably and clenched his jaw. 'Something like that, I guess.'

Two plump, middle-aged women were setting out plastic plates with sandwiches and bowls of cut-up fruit. One of them looked at Isaac with undisguised curiosity, a huge smile stretching across her face.

'Tessa, is this your fiancé? We get to meet him at last.' She nodded at Isaac, her eyes roving over him appreciatively. 'You're the best kept secret in town, Paul,' she told him. 'Although I understand now why Tessa wanted to keep you all to herself.'

'No, Hilda,' Tessa said, appalled not so much by the woman's mistake as the amused gleam in Isaac's eyes. 'This isn't Paul. This is my—my brother, Isaac.'

'Oh.' Hilda was clearly disappointed.

'I'll be back in time to settle the children for their afternoon naps,' Tessa added, guiding Isaac to the door.

They stepped through the front doorway past the simple painted sign that said, Preschool Director Theresa Morrow. It seemed that Isaac couldn't help flinging her a bitter taunt.

'What do you think you're doing here? Playing at being another Mother Teresa?'

Tessa flinched. Surely he'd hurt her enough? Where was all this bitterness coming from? 'I thought you, of all people, would understand,' she replied softly. 'These children deserve just as good a start as those from well-off families.'

'Well, of course,' he growled, apparently not liking her answer. 'I guess, as you said, I just wasn't prepared to find you doing this kind of work.'

'Well, maybe it won't last much longer.' Tessa sighed. 'The land in this area has been increasing in value recently. I've heard it rumoured that property developers have their eye on it. We won't stand a chance if they decide to make a move. But apart from that, Paul doesn't approve of my work here at all. He wants me to apply for a job with a properly run government or private kindergarten next year. This is only a poorly subsidised charity affair, and he is most uncomfortable at the thought of having his wife in such a lowly position.'

'He regards his own position in this town's social hierarchy very dearly?'

Tessa sighed, 'Yes, of course.'

'And how do you feel about his attitude?'

It was a fair question, but it was one Tessa had avoided facing. Whenever Paul had pestered her about leaving her job, she had changed the subject, making it clear that she didn't want to discuss it. But she knew that when they returned from their honeymoon and she went back to work, Paul would remount his campaign to have her re-sign. But there was no way she would tell Isaac that.

'Actually,' she said, shooting him an arch smile, 'I thought I might be able to sweet-talk him around to my way of thinking.'

But somehow she gained the distinct impression that wasn't the answer he'd wanted to hear.

They drove to the The Quarterdeck, a restaurant on the seafront overlooking the marina. As they crossed the timber decking, the tropical winter sun was strong enough to encourage them to find a table in a section protected by a white canvas sail stretched overhead. They both ordered pumpkin damper with a Greek salad and lemon-flavoured mineral water.

Isaac cleared his throat. 'If we're going to set the record straight, the first thing I should probably admit to you,' he began as soon as the orders were placed, 'is that I have been in contact with your father over the years.'

He couldn't have startled Tessa more if he had told her he had three weeks to live.

'Really?' she asked at last. 'He never said—'

'I asked him not to,' he interrupted, then paused as the waiter returned with their drinks. 'But I couldn't hurt a man who has been so good to me by just rudely walking out on him without some indication of my gratitude.'

But you could hurt me and deceive me without any qualms! Fighting back tears, Tessa twirled the straw in her glass, making the ice-cubes clink. She wanted to cry. Her father had deceived her for all that time. How could he? What was so wrong with her that everyone conspired against her? Her eyes, blurred by hot tears, scanned the rows of yachts moored in the marina. Was this her punishment for behaving like a wanton woman at the tender age of nineteen?

'Did he know you were going to leave?' She had to ask but could hardly bear to hear the answer.

'Oh, no, not at all. He had no part in it.'

Tessa took a deep breath. She had promised herself she wouldn't stoop so low as to ask one particular question, but her self-control was almost in tatters. 'I have to know, Isaac. How could you walk out on me after all those…times? Isaac, what happened to make you suddenly so mad at me that you had to run away?'

He took a long swig of his drink and sighed. Her hands were so tightly clenched Tessa could feel her fingernails digging into her palms.

'It wasn't just one thing, Tess. It was everything about us. We were so different from each other we might as well have grown up in separate countries.'

'But we didn't,' she cried. 'We weren't brought up at opposite ends of the earth. We grew up in the same house. We had an incredible lot in common. We—we were lovers.' Her voice broke on the last word, and pink crept into her cheeks.

He drained his drink in a swift gulp, and the ice crashed to the bottom of his glass.

'We were very young,' he told her. 'Our hormones were pretty rampant.'

'Are you telling me that's all there was between us? Adolescent hormones?'

'Perhaps.' He shrugged, pulling a wry face, pretending bewilderment. 'I mean it just kind of evolved, didn't it? You know—one minute you were my kid sister, all skinny and hopeless at cricket, and the next you turned into this—' he smiled at her gently '—incredibly beautiful woman.'

Their meals arrived, and there was a long silence as they unrolled knives and forks from paper serviettes and tasted the food.

'See how even the waiter couldn't take his eyes off you?'

'You mean I grew into some kind of wicked temptress?'

'No,' he said. 'I can't really blame you.'

'I'm glad to hear it,' retorted Tessa.

'But then again,' he continued with a lazy grin, 'you were the one whose legs changed from gangly to honeygold shapely in just one summer.' His eyes slid to her breasts. 'And other attributes emerged—with a suddenness that robbed me of my commonsense.'

Tessa rolled her eyes. 'I'm not going to even *begin* to apologise for growing up! Of all the lame, chauvinist excuses!' Exasperated, she pushed the barely touched salad away from her and folded her arms. Then her face softened as she remembered. 'I was pretty gone on you from a very young age, so I guess it was partly my fault.'

'Your hero-worship was what kept me going through the late high school years. Remember when I wanted to drop out and hang around with the gangs in back alleys or on street corners? But the thought of going on to university with you, of making something of myself, was like a talisman.'

He smiled a slow, sexy smile that melted her insides. Tessa leaned forward. 'There were many times when I did sneak away in the hope of finding you alone on the hill.' She smiled sheepishly.

'There were?' he asked with mock surprise. 'I thought you were just interested in keeping fit like I was—jogging up and down that blessed goat track for training. No wonder we both ended up cross-country champions.'

'I only won that first year. I'm afraid my fitness dete
riorated after—'

'After I kissed you?'

'We did a lot less jogging after that.'

But there was plenty of other physical activity, she remembered. Not that they'd completed the act they'd so
naively begun until some time later. They'd been shy and
just a little frightened at first, tentatively exploring a new
and secret world. She'd no idea a boy could be so tender
and sweet.

'It was so difficult to carry on at home as if nothing
was happening,' commented Isaac.

'I think we did our best to behave just as we always
had, but I remember Mum became even more reserved
towards you.'

A black shadow crossed swiftly over Isaac's sharp features. 'And your father subtly suggested that I spend more
of my spare time with the "young men" in the area, playing football or sailing. In fact it was actually your dad's
idea that I spend those two entire summer holidays away
from home fruit picking around Bowen and Charters
Towers.'

'I hated that,' remembered Tessa. 'I got so bored with
the other kids in the neighbourhood. But at least you
saved enough to have those scuba diving lessons when
you started university.'

'Yeah.' Isaac sighed. 'At university we suddenly had
all that freedom....'

Tessa's drink ended in an unexpected slurp, and she
looked up to find his eyes on her.

He frowned. 'We were still far too young.'

'Well, obviously we weren't. We went ahead and—I
think we scared my parents out of their wits.' Tessa
smiled.

Then she wondered just what she'd said to make Isaac's face harden so quickly. He scrunched his serviette into a tiny ball and flung it down hard on his plate.

'And they had every reason to worry,' he muttered through compressed lips. 'Their baby princess cavorting with a tramp.'

'You make us sound like a Walt Disney movie,' she countered.

'Our situation was just as unreal.'

Tessa's breath caught in her throat. 'Unreal? It was incredibly real to me, Isaac.'

'Was it?' he asked, as he leant back in his chair and took a long, deep breath.

When she dragged her eyes away from the breadth of Isaac's shoulders and the shadowy hint of dark hair at the opening of his shirt, Tessa saw once again that his dark, brooding eyes were veiled by a weary sadness, as if the past nine years had provided him with far too many harsh experiences.

He grimaced. 'I'm afraid that when you're young, the line between reality and fantasy, between sense and sensibility, keeps moving. You can't get a handle on it. You begin to think the impossible really is possible.'

Tessa sat in silence, staring past Isaac for a very long time. A seagull swooped in the blue air behind him, and she watched it dive and soar as she considered his words. Had their relationship been impossible? It had always seemed quite possible to her. Of course, Rosalind would have been a problem. But not an insurmountable one, surely?

'Do you think if we'd met again now, as adults, it would have been different?'

'Well, yes, of course it would be different. You're already deeply involved with another man.'

An icy horror clamped tightly inside her, catching at her breath. Talk about fantasy and reality, possibility and impossibility! She had almost, for a few senseless minutes, completely forgotten about Paul! Where on earth had her deviate mind been travelling?

'I was—was just speaking hypothetically.' She waved a hand, airily trying to dismiss the conversation. 'How silly of me. It's just that sometimes, when you look back on things—you see how perhaps one word, one gesture, one question at the right moment might have changed your whole future.'

'Tessa, the one thing we don't need now is hindsight. We are not going to change anything.'

She couldn't hold back the pitifully weak cry. 'Would you like to, Isaac?'

His chair scraped on the wooden deck as he jerked it back. He couldn't have looked more alarmed if he were a politician who'd discovered his table had been bugged.

'For God's sake, Tessa. Of course not.'

How had she been so weak? Of all the inane questions! She looked at her hands trembling in her lap. The fact that she'd given this man her virginity, her dreams, herself, only to have him turn his back on her and walk away forever made her want to yell at him. She would feel so much better if she could hurl the large white plate covered in half-eaten salad straight at him and make a terrible scene. Make him see what he'd done to her. What a mess she'd become.

What had they achieved by discussing the past?

Despite her quivering chin, Tessa managed to speak with determined cool. 'Do you consider we've set things sufficiently straight? I must get back to work.' Her hand strayed to her hair.

'You don't wear your engagement ring to work?' he

asked unexpectedly, his dark eyes resting on the tendril of golden hair wound around her finger.

'No. It's not really suitable,' she replied. 'Emeralds are soft. They scratch or fracture easily.' She slipped a slender gold chain from beneath her blouse. The ring was hanging from it.

She blushed as Isaac allowed a smouldering gaze to linger on her blouse where it fell to a V over her breasts.

'An enchanting and fitting repository,' he murmured. 'I'm sure Paul must be delighted that the token of his devotion to you has such a charming home.'

With bright pink cheeks, she looked at her watch. 'I really must get back to work.'

'Of course.' He stood quickly and tried to help her out of her chair, but Tessa was too fast. She didn't want him to touch her. In her haste, she found herself ploughing into him. First her shoulder and then her chin, followed swiftly by her lips, met the cotton knit of his shirt and his muscles beneath in a rapid, unstoppable succession.

'Steady!' he cried as his arms came around to balance her.

Don't look up! her mind warned even as her traitorous eyes lifted to find his.

A mistake!

For when her gaze met his dark eyes inches above hers, she saw something that sliced into her soul. She saw and knew instinctively that Isaac was hurting to have her so close. In the black depths of his eyes she could read hunger, pain and desperate need. A need that mirrored her own, raw and defenceless. A need that made her rise on tiptoes, wind her hands around his neck and press more closely into him, her lips parted in eager invitation.

But he stepped away from her.

She didn't have time to be embarrassed by his rejection.

Almost instantly she realised that he was distracted by
someone whose footsteps sounded on the boardwalk behind her.

'Paul,' Isaac said, looking over Tessa's shoulder. 'Good
to see you again.'

CHAPTER FOUR

FOR ridiculous seconds, the three of them didn't move or speak. The absurd thought flashed through Tessa's mind that they looked like a freeze frame of the eternal triangle. Isaac was glaring silently, Paul stood open-mouthed, and she could feel the flush on her cheeks spreading to the roots of her hair.

She had embarrassed everyone!

Isaac had done absolutely nothing to invite her demonstrative response. Throwing herself at him yet again was unjustifiable on any grounds. And Paul had done nothing to merit her betrayal.

There was no doubt she deserved the horrific sense of utter disgrace that overwhelmed her. And she deserved Paul's white-faced shock. What she didn't deserve was the neat way Isaac rescued the situation.

'You must forgive me, Paul,' he said quickly, giving the other man a comforting pat on the shoulder. 'I brought Tessa out to lunch and then talked her into having a champagne cocktail for old times' sake. I should have known after the fainting spell yesterday that alcohol at lunch could go straight to her head.'

While Tessa assimilated Isaac's bald-faced lie, Paul's bewildered expression relaxed slightly.

'Tessa doesn't usually drink much at all.'

'That's right,' agreed Isaac. 'She told me that, but foolishly I insisted. She seemed fine until she stood up, and then she had a little trouble staying on two feet.'

'But I'll be all right now, thank you, Isaac,' said Tessa,

stepping away from him and flashing a wan smile at her fiancé. 'Are you about to have lunch, Paul?' she asked him, noticing with relief that he had closed his gaping mouth.

'Yes. I'm here with colleagues.' He indicated a table some distance away at which were seated several men in neat grey suits identical to his. 'Are you fit to return to work, Tessa?' he asked, his eyes narrowing as he reached into his breast pocket. To Tessa's discomfort, Paul swiftly donned his spectacles and scrutinised her closely as if searching for clear evidence of her crime. *Any minute now he'll be sniffing my breath,* she thought. 'You do look rather flushed, my dear,' he said slowly.

'I—I think I'll be fine now, thanks, Paul,' she replied, feeling distinctly heavy-hearted and anything but all right. She was sure she must be shaking visibly. 'I really must get back to the preschool. I've overstayed my time.'

'Yes,' replied Paul, his lip curling into a sneer. 'I'm sure you have something very demanding to do there, like watching over the dear little things while they take their naps.'

Tessa decided she wasn't really in a position to take offence at Paul's snide remark. 'Will you be coming to dinner tonight?' she asked him politely. 'My grandmother is arriving from Sydney this afternoon. I know she'd love to see you again before the wed—before Saturday.'

'I'd certainly like to meet her,' said Paul. He stepped forward and kissed Tessa's cheek. 'I'll see you this evening then, my sweet.' Then he added abruptly, 'Good day, Isaac.' He nodded curtly at them both and returned to his table.

Tessa tried to walk sedately with head high and back straight, but she felt sure her gait was more of a stumble as she silently crossed the deck beside Isaac. It occurred to her that if Paul were watching, he would be quite certain she really was tipsy. Isaac would probably be thinking that she was a good actress, while she found herself wondering if she was experiencing the first symptoms of a nervous breakdown.

They reached the car park where Isaac's truck was parked under a tree with Devil waiting patiently in the back.

'I should have brought him a doggy bag,' Tessa offered as Isaac paused briefly to give his dog's head a swift rub.

'He doesn't need feeding in the middle of the day,' he said coldly. 'And he has enough water.'

He opened the door for her.

'Thank you so much for helping me out, Isaac,' she said.

He didn't reply.

His silence was upsetting, and his black eyes could not have been harder or more unsmiling if he had been her executioner. He closed the door sharply after Tessa was seated and marched swiftly to the driver's side. He opened his door, then swung into his seat and ignited the engine in one smooth motion.

'I really am sorry,' she said. 'I—I'm sorry you had to lie to cover for me.'

The booted foot pressed down firmly on the accelerator, and the truck lurched forward.

Tessa felt so wretched, so ill and so desperate, she needed his absolution. 'Isaac, please at least accept my apology.'

'I'd rather not discuss this,' he muttered through clenched teeth, and his fist, as it gripped the gear stick, showed white knuckles. The truck's engine roared as he sped, grim-faced and silent, along the bitumen.

Outside the Burrawang centre, Tessa stepped from the vehicle.

'You finish at five?' he snapped.

'Yes. If you like I could ring Paul and ask him to pick me up.'

'That sounds sensible—a diplomatic gesture,' he said quietly and then quickly jerked his eyes away from her to stare through the windscreen.

'Thanks for the lunch, Isaac.'

He nodded without looking at her, his profile still utterly formidable and the line of his mouth so firmly unyielding she felt afraid of him. And perhaps just a little afraid *for* him. He looked so fierce and so determined, as if he planned murder.

Then the ignition was fired again, and the black truck took off with a snarl of its motor, showering her in a cloud of dust from the roadside gravel. From the back of the truck, Devil sent her a reproving bark.

Tessa had never felt so rejected, so alone. She knew it was completely irrational that she still cared what Isaac thought of her. She should be grateful that he saved her face in front of Paul. But all she could think of was how his return had reinforced the utter hopelessness of her burning need for him, while he carried not even a thimbleful of such feeling for her.

Late afternoon sun slanted through the timber shutters as Lydia Burnie stood in the Morrows' lounge, her granddaughter's hand clasped in her thin grip, while she gazed with delighted amusement at the pile of wedding presents on the long mahogany coffee table.

'My goodness, Tessa, dear,' exclaimed Lydia. 'This certainly looks like a house where things are happening.'

The unopened gifts looked tasteful and tempting in their white, gold or silver wrappings.

'When are you and Paul going to start opening all these lovely things?'

'Probably this evening, Grandma, although they look so pretty as they are, don't they?' replied Tessa.

'Well, my dear, they certainly match the rest of Rosalind's decor. Anyone could be forgiven for thinking the wedding was going to be held at home here.'

Tessa smiled as her eyes circled the room, taking in all Rosalind's efforts to produce bridal finery. 'Mum certainly has been going overboard in the decorating department,' she admitted. 'But most of these things are going to be transferred to the marquee in Queen's Gardens to make the reception look more bridal. Would you like me to show you all the things she has ready?' she asked gently, slipping her arm through her grandmother's.

'I never was one for too much fuss and bother,' murmured Lydia, 'but I know it can be very important to others.'

Tessa led her towards the enormous sideboard piled with all manner of exquisite items. 'Each guest will receive one of these little pink organza sachets filled with gold-covered almonds and heart-shaped chocolates,' Tessa began. 'Mum has filled all those herself.'

'How sweet,' murmured Lydia, in a dry, unreadable tone.

'She's making this wedding as close to a fairy-tale affair as she can, isn't she?' Lydia whispered loudly.

Tessa had been about to show her grandmother the Casablanca lilies that would be used in the church. She broke into a thin, slightly cracked laugh. 'It looks that way, doesn't it?'

'You should be absolutely delighted, you lucky girl.'

'Of course.'

'But sweetheart, you're not, are you?'

Tessa shot her grandmother a swift, searching glance. 'I am, Grandma. It's all going to be so beautiful.'

'I'm not talking about this finery, Theresa Rose, and you know it. You know exactly what I'm talking about. You don't look like a woman who's about to marry the man of her dreams.'

Lydia's firm grasp on Tessa's arm prevented her from pulling away as she wanted to. She couldn't handle this conversation. Not after the ordeal of lunch. Not after the greater ordeal of Isaac's arrival. But she had no choice. She was held captive by a frail old woman of eighty-seven, and unexpectedly by her own need to answer the question. It suddenly became vitally important to Tessa to justify marrying Paul—to her grandmother and to herself.

'Grandma, we both know that very few women ever meet the man of their dreams, let alone marry him.'

Lydia pursed her lips and scrutinised Tessa with narrowed eyes. 'Humph!' she exclaimed. 'I hope your mother hasn't fed you that hogwash.'

'What's that, darling?' interrupted Rosalind, breezing into the room, her arms full of delicate trails of green ivy. 'Isn't this lovely? It's from the garden, and there's heaps more. I think I'll use some on the church pews.'

'Well, that will be one saving,' muttered Lydia.

'Did you know that ivy is the symbol of friendship and fidelity in marriage?' Rosalind asked them as she added trails of greenery to the urn of lilies.

'Fidelity and friendship?' Lydia echoed.

'The two most important elements in marriage,' answered Rosalind. 'And we have no doubts about Paul's capacity for fidelity or friendship,' she added.

'I suppose they make a possible substitute.' Lydia sighed.

The two other women stared at her. Tessa willed her grandmother to be quiet. Rosalind asked in a waspish voice, 'Substitute? Mother, what on earth are you talking about?'

'I'm talking about old-fashioned romance, hot-blooded passion, *sex*. Whatever you want to call it, it's what I've always understood lies at the heart of a good marriage.'

'Mother! I've never heard you talk like this before. All that—that sort of thing is understood, of course.' Rosalind was flushed and almost spluttering.

'Humph!' grumbled Lydia again. 'Are the men out on the deck?' she asked Tessa. 'Take me out there for a breath of fresh air, please, my dear.'

Tessa completely understood her grandmother's need for fresh air. As she assisted Lydia onto the deck, her chest was so painfully tight that she feared for her next breath.

Her father and Paul were standing at the far rail and staring out to sea. Tessa helped Lydia make herself comfortable in a straight-backed chair. She poured her a glass of her favourite sweet sherry from the drinks trolley, then excused herself and crossed the deck to join the men. They were staring at something on the bay.

'What's so interesting?' she asked.

'We're just watching Isaac out there with *Antares*,' replied her father. 'He's been ploughing up and down that bay for the last hour as if his life depends on it.'

Tessa stood beside John Morrow. The bay was choppy, whipped to little white-capped peaks by southerly breezes. There were several sailing boats out on the water, but she found the familiar, sleek lines of the family's sloop, *Antares*, immediately. The yacht was streaking through the water. And the sight of it made her heart flutter helplessly like a very timid bird in a cage.

A few minutes earlier, when she was inside with Lydia looking at the gifts, the flowers and all the beautiful accessories, her wedding to Paul had seemed a reality—a distinct possibility. Despite Lydia's mutterings, Tessa had almost felt safe and secure at the promise of Paul as a faithful and friendly husband.

But short moments later, watching Isaac force *Antares* to the far reach of her capacity and remembering the murderous fury of his face when he left her after lunch, nothing seemed safe or sane. Isaac spelled danger, and yet every nerve of her body longed to be out there with him, testing the elements and the boat's strength, feeling the rough wind in her face and hair, joining him in the cabin below....

As she had when she was nineteen.

'He'll have to bring her in soon or he'll be late for dinner,' John Morrow said.

'When has that ever bothered Isaac?' taunted Paul. 'Who's for another drink? What can I get you, Tessa? Maybe you'd better have a soft drink, my dear.'

'Of course,' replied Tessa, who'd been feeling the need for something far stronger.

She refused to look at the bay again, and with her glass of lemon squash took a seat beside her grandmother. Lydia chattered happily enough about the garden in her small home unit and complained about her noisy neighbours while Tessa pretended to listen. But the image of Isaac sailing sent her mind shooting into the past, and she could no more halt its unravelling than she could command the earth to stop spinning.

Antares had crossed the bay in record time on that July Saturday afternoon ten years ago. She and Isaac were proud of their trim sailing as they tacked close to Magnetic Island, skimmed past Arcadia and headed into beautiful Florence Bay. The water sparkled as blue and clear as any photo in a tourist brochure. And the beach before them curved like a freshly peeled banana, pale and smooth and untouched.

As they dropped anchor, Tessa called to Isaac, 'I'm sure the Mediterranean couldn't be any more beautiful than this. Remember we used to read all those Greek myths and legends?' She tilted her head back to let the mild winter sun stream over her face and stretched her long, smooth, golden-brown legs to take in more of the sunshine. 'Actually,' she added with a frown, 'some of those stories were ridiculously far-fetched.'

'How do you mean?' Isaac called as he finished reefing the sail. He jumped into the cockpit.

Tessa looked at him. With his dark hair a little too long and wild from the wind and with his chest bare and suntanned, his tattered denim shorts hanging loosely from his hips, he looked absolutely perfect to her—as heroic as any legendary character. And his dark eyes were hungrily taking in the length and shapeliness of her limbs, just as she'd hoped.

'Remember that story about Calypso who lived on a remote island? She was a goddess and she was supposed to be absolutely drop dead gorgeous. And yet, when the Greek hero Ulysses landed on her island and stayed with her all that time—lived alone with her for seven whole years—they never...you know...'

Isaac stared at her, his dark eyes stern and frowning. Then his lips twisted into a teasing smile. 'They never what?'

Tessa blushed. 'They never did *it*—anything.'

'You mean they never made love?'

She nodded.

'He was supposed to stay faithful to his wife, wasn't he?'

'As if!' Tessa retorted scornfully. She was about to expand on the impossibility of such a situation when an unexpected fierce heat that flared in Isaac's eyes startled her.

'It's not so unbelievable,' he said quietly.

Tessa sat up straighter, tingling with a sudden sense of anticipation. Instinctively, she guessed what Isaac was thinking and her pulses began to race.

'I know someone who's done that,' he said softly, his gaze not leaving hers.

'What do you mean?' she asked, her heart jerking uncomfortably. 'Who are you talking about?'

He edged towards her with the grace and stealth of a magnificent wild cat. 'I know this guy who's lived with an incredibly beautiful girl with golden hair and the sexiest legs in all history for almost seven years.' He paused, and his eyes, as they held hers, were polished ebony.

'And?' she asked, her voice wobbling over the simple syllable.

'And he's been crazy about her all this time and hasn't done anything.'

The afternoon was still and silent. The only sounds were the gentle lapping of the waves around *Antares*'s sparkling white hull, the occasional clinking of the halyards against the mast—and the thudding of Tessa's heartbeat.

'Does he know how *she* feels?' she managed to ask, wishing she didn't feel so nervous, as if her whole life depended on the next few seconds.

He reached out a long brown arm, and his fingers lifted

a strand of her hair. 'It's making her pretty edgy, I think,' he said, his voice deep and rough.

Tessa's fingers strayed to her hair, and his hand clasped hers tightly. 'He should probably do something about it,' she whispered.

Isaac's hand released hers, and his finger circled her ear lobe, sending shivers racing down her neck. 'He's been waiting for the right moment.' The delicious shivers urged her to lean towards him, to rest her head on his chest where she could hear his heart pounding as fiercely as hers.

'If he waits too long,' she murmured as Isaac's strong arms closed around her, 'the same thing might happen to him as happened to Ulysses.'

'What was that?' he asked with a soft laugh, his lips in her hair.

'The gods sent him packing off Calypso's island and on his way home. Calypso was left behind. She missed out completely.'

She tried to laugh, but the stormy expression on Isaac's face froze the response. 'Not even the gods could ever make me leave you, Queen Tess,' he muttered savagely. 'But just in case they try—' He kissed her swiftly before scooping her up in his arms and hurrying with her to the companionway that led to the cabin below.

Tessa laughed. 'Isaac, put me down! You can't carry me down that little ladder. We'll both break our necks, and then we'll never—' She slipped out of Isaac's arms and scurried down the ladder as quickly as a wild creature disappearing into its burrow.

Isaac was close behind, and they tumbled in a breathless, laughing heap onto the main cabin's bunk. All nervousness or hesitancy vanished. It was amazing how right it fell as Isaac slipped off her cotton T-shirt to reveal her tiny pink bikini top.

Tessa lay still, her body suffused with an overwhelming longing.

His lips descended to trail over the small pink triangles. 'Pretty in pink,' he whispered as he untied the string behind her neck and peeled the fabric away. His breath caught at the sight of her breasts, her nipples urgently peaking for his attention. 'Oh, Tess, these are much prettier pinks.'

And there was very little talking after that.

They hadn't been all that good at lovemaking that first time, Tessa remembered with a slow smile. They had both been so in awe of the sweet discovery of each other's bodies and so overwhelmed by the shocking power of newly unleashed desires. But they had felt very clever very quickly. Soon they were convinced that they were, without doubt, the world's hottest young lovers.

And it had never, not once, felt wrong.

A shadow fell across Tessa. Lydia was leaning over to speak quite loudly in her ear. 'My dear, could you help me up? I would like to visit the bathroom before dinner.'

Startled, Tessa stared at her grandmother, at her empty sherry glass and at her untouched glass of lemon squash. 'I must have been daydreaming,' she apologised, jumping up to assist her grandmother.

'So I noticed,' replied Lydia, clutching at Tessa's strong, young arm as she stood up stiffly. 'Perhaps I was wrong before,' she commented as they headed inside the house. 'The look on your face just now suggests that perhaps you are deeply in love, after all. I must say, my dear, I'm relieved.'

'That's good,' whispered Tessa, but her throat closed

tightly over any other comment she might have forced
herself to offer.

Isaac was late for dinner.

The air was decidedly chilled as he entered the dining
room. Tessa's parents, her grandmother, Paul and she
were all assembled and had almost finished their main
course—Rosalind's minted Victorian lamb cutlets with
three kinds of vegetables—as Isaac apologised for his
lateness before lowering himself into the only vacant
chair.

'I'll just go and heat up your meal now that you're
here,' Rosalind said without the faintest trace of a smile.

'Thank you, Rosalind,' Isaac replied, his voice mellow
with studied politeness.

'You may as well heat up Theresa's, as well,' interjected Lydia. 'She's hardly touched her food. It's sure to
have gone cold.'

The eyes of everyone at the table swung to Tessa,
whose lashes lowered as she stared at her plate.

'Tessa had rather a large lunch today.' Paul had a gal-
lant smile for his fiancée beside him. He patted her hand,
and she quickly picked up her fork, speared a baby carrot
and bit into it.

But she immediately regretted her swift reaction. The
lift of Isaac's eyebrow told her he hadn't missed the speed
with which she'd retracted her hand from Paul's touch.

'So you and Tessa had lunch together,' her father was
saying to Paul. 'How nice. I never seem to be free for
lunch these days.'

'Well, actually, Tessa had lunch with Isaac,' said Paul,
and then he looked around, clearly a trifle embarrassed.

*Paul is not exactly exercising his incisive legal mind
tonight*, thought Tessa. There was no need for him to let

that little item of news slip. Neither she nor Isaac was likely to broadcast details of their lunch.

She saw Isaac's wary glance shoot to Rosalind, who had returned with his meal. Her mother looked suddenly pale, but her eyes met his with a challenging glitter as she said, 'Of course, what a lovely idea for these two to dine out together. They are, after all, brother and sister.'

'What are you talking about, Rosalind Morrow?' asked Lydia. 'Isaac and your Tessa are no more brother and sister than—than Romeo and Juliet.'

Tessa almost choked on a floret of broccoli. She grabbed her wineglass and took a swift swig. 'Grandma, for heaven's sake,' she gasped.

The jet-black flash of anger in Isaac's eyes made breathing difficult, and the tight, stunned expression on Paul's face wasn't helping, either.

'Time to open another bottle while Isaac enjoys his dinner,' Dr. Morrow said with a small laugh, and everyone seemed grateful for the distraction.

The glasses were topped up and conversation began to flow more easily. Except that Tessa noticed the conversation kept returning to Isaac. It was as if he sat in the hot seat. Paul, continuing to help himself to the red wine, asked endless questions about Isaac's mining company, about the environmental threats of mining and even the issue of Aboriginal land rights. But rarely did Tessa feel the questions were prompted by genuine interest.

She was as mystified and curious as anybody else in the room about how Isaac had filled in the past nine years in Western Australia, but her fiancé's probing, impolite inquisition appalled her.

And she could tell Isaac was annoyed. By the time they reached dessert—liquered fruits in vanilla bean custard—

it seemed more like he was a prisoner on trial for rape or murder than a house guest, however unexpected.

Spurred on perhaps by the wine, Paul warmed to the task of firing unsettling questions. His round face grew pink with concentration. Tessa could tell Isaac's tolerance level was dropping. A fixed jaw held his smile in place, and his dark head tilted sharply.

'Paul,' she whispered, unable to bear any more. Her fiancé turned to her, his face flushed and animated. 'I think you've asked Isaac enough pointed questions for one evening.'

'What do you mean, Tessa? You can't trust these mining companies. They could sell our country from right under our noses if we don't watch them carefully.'

Tessa saw Isaac's fist clench around the stem of his wineglass. 'Tessa's right,' he said very softly. 'These questions are hardly suitable topics for dinner. But in my defence, I must make it clear that my negotiations with Pantex Mining and Global Austral are quite clearly to Australia's advantage.' His voice dropped. 'But if you want to keep pushing this issue, Hammond, I should warn you that we miners have been known to settle our debates out on the grass.'

There was a startled gasp around the table. Tessa had a sudden vision of Isaac quietly decking Paul and tipping him over the verandah into the thorny bougainvillea below.

She couldn't let herself dwell on that thought.

'I've been telling Tessa she should open some of those lovely wedding presents,' said Lydia.

There was a relieved murmur of assent around the table.

'That would be nice. We could watch while we have coffee,' agreed Rosalind, underlining her words with a forced brightness.

Isaac and Paul glared at each other for a few seconds longer, and then everyone stood, relieved to leave the table.

The opening of the gifts was a pleasant enough affair. There were beautiful presents that had been delivered from out of town, not to mention the delicate linen from Lydia, the Wedgwood bone china from Rosalind and John and the Waterford crystal glasses from Paul's parents. But Tessa wished wholeheartedly that, when Paul hugged her with delight at the sight of so many generous gifts, she'd felt even a fraction of the adrenalin rush caused by Isaac's black-eyed gaze briefly linking with hers across the room.

But what really spoiled the evening was another question from Paul.

'Isaac,' he said silkily, as he carefully placed his empty cup and saucer on the table. 'Do you have a present for the bride-to-be?'

'Of course not,' Tessa interrupted rather too loudly, so that at first she didn't take in Isaac's soft reply.

'Indeed I do.'

She stared at him open-mouthed as he stood slowly, with magnificent dignity. Did she imagine the haughty straightening of his shoulders? The obvious lift of his jaw? He looked at the circle of expectant faces before his eyes rested for the longest time on her as she stood in the middle of the room. 'If you'll excuse me, I'll get my gift.'

CHAPTER FIVE

TESSA would not have been surprised if Isaac had simply kept on walking when he left the room. 'Paul, there was no need to embarrass Isaac like that,' she said angrily.

'Embarrass Isaac?' scoffed Paul. 'That guy has the hide of a rhinoceros. Nothing would faze him. Anyhow, he can't just suddenly turn up here now, out of the blue, and not expect to comply with some of the basic social conventions—like a gift for the bride, at least.'

'Make sure all the cards are with the right gifts so you remember whom to thank,' Rosalind intervened, and Tessa was grateful to have a task to distract her from mulling over the present Isaac was fetching.

She was kneeling on the floor tucking Aunt Mary's card into a covered vegetable dish delicately trimmed with gold, when navy blue deck shoes and long legs encased in blue jeans approached across the carpet and stopped just in front of her.

Why, she wondered with a surge of helplessness, was she shaking? Why did she suddenly want to cry? Why had the past come back to haunt her now, just when she was on the verge of starting afresh?

'Here, let me help you up, Tessa.' She heard Paul's voice. 'Let's see Isaac's surprise.'

Isaac was holding one small package and a large box-shaped parcel. 'I have something basic and practical,' Isaac said with a grin, presenting the larger gift to Paul. 'And something special for Tessa—' he paused and cleared his throat '—because she always was a very special foster sister to me.' He placed the small package in Tessa's trembling hand. His dark eyes smouldered and held hers momentarily as he bent forward and placed a swift, brotherly kiss on her cheek.

She stared at the neat rectangular parcel wrapped in stiff white paper dotted with silver bells, and she found herself wondering absurdly whether Isaac had wrapped it or if it had been wrapped in a store by some wide-eyed assistant.

'Open the big one first,' cried her father with a wink that was almost Tessa's undoing.

'Yes, Paul,' she agreed. 'Let's have a look at what you've got.'

The present was indeed functional—a stainless steel electric kettle, the kind that combined practicality with impressive modern design.

'Can't start the day without a cuppa. Good call, Isaac,' cheered Lydia.

Tessa added her thanks. Paul looked flushed and a trifle embarrassed.

'What's in yours, Tessa?' asked Lydia.

The room seemed incredibly silent as Tessa began to peel back the sticky tape on her gift. Her shaking fingers made the job almost impossible.

'Oh, no,' Isaac said with a tight smile. 'I've just re-membered how long you used to take opening birthday presents, trying so hard not to tear the paper. Just rip it open, Tess.'

'I'm trying,' she whispered. It was all the sound she could manage. And then her task was made even more difficult by the sudden blurring of her vision. She had to wipe her eyes with the back of her hand.

The onlookers watched in unhelpful silence.

'Here, let me,' said Isaac gently. He took the package from her trembling grasp and tore the paper away. Inside was a flat white box, which he flipped open with his thumb.

'Oh, it's jewellery,' breathed Lydia. 'How lovely.'

Isaac lifted out his gift. It was an exquisite, heart-shaped solid gold pendant encrusted with pearls on a beautiful short gold chain.

'A keepsake,' Lydia said, gushing. 'How *romantic*.'

Rosalind glared at her mother.

'Isaac,' whispered Tessa. 'Oh, Isaac.' She looked at the assembled people and wished she could make every one of them—including Paul—vanish with a flick of her fingers. How could she hide her feelings for Isaac in the face of such thoughtfulness?

But, if his thoughtful gift caused her anguish, there was worse to come.

'Is that Western Australian gold?' asked Dr. Morrow.

'Yes.' Isaac's chin came up, and he fixed his level gaze on his foster father. But, Tessa noted, his hand, which held the pendant, shook ever so slightly. 'This is made from the very first gold I found when I started prospecting in the Pilbara. I've saved it for a special...' He cleared his throat. 'A very special occasion.'

Then he fastened the pendant around Tessa's neck and stepped back, his dark eyes softening as they rested on the heart lying against her white throat. 'I knew it would look lovely on you,' he said softly. 'I don't know if this suits your wedding dress or not, but you're welcome to wear it on the big day if you like.'

If I like! Tessa wanted to cry. *Oh, Isaac! How could I like to wear your gift while I marry someone else!* She couldn't bear it. Couldn't bear the soft, sad glow in his eyes as he looked at her, or the memory of his fingers warm on her neck as he fastened the clasp, or the thought of him keeping that gold all those years. And especially

she couldn't hear the startled hush of her family and fiancé
as they witnessed this exhibition.

It was a gesture that might once have spelled lasting,
glorious happiness but now could only bring disaster and
anguish to everyone present. Unless she was very brave.

Unless she managed to hide completely her breaking
heart.

With great effort, she turned away from Isaac to face
Paul. Her fiancé was looking a little shaken. He smiled at
her weakly then looked at the rest of her wide-eyed family. 'I suppose Isaac also travelled to Broome to skindive
for the pearls himself, as well,' he said with a bitter laugh
that began to teeter slightly out of control.

Tessa ground her teeth in annoyance. Surely Isaac had
been forced to field enough snide remarks for one evening. She sincerely doubted his ability to tolerate Paul's
nervous laughter, which even to her generous ears
sounded rather desperate and mildly asthmatic.

But Tessa knew it was useless to allow her sympathy
for Isaac to tug at her heartstrings. The entire family was
watching her with wary curiosity. Her only option was to
slip her arm through Paul's and beam her brightest smile
at him as if he'd been the one who'd just presented her
with a gift at least as expensive and beautiful as the Taj
Mahal.

She hated to turn her back on Isaac while his beautiful
heart lay resting against the base of her throat, but it was
the only sane course of action. She reminded herself that
he had stopped thinking of her as his own woman years
ago. This was the exact scenario he had come to witness.
It was time to give him exactly what he expected.

But it hurt.

It hurt to watch him stand to one side, to see the way
he avoided looking at her and how he forced a polite smile

for the others. And it felt no better to see him refuse Rosalind's offer of a second cup of coffee before gathering some of the cups and saucers people had finished with and carrying them to the kitchen.

'I have a phone call to make, if you'll excuse me,' he said over his shoulder as he left.

Of course he didn't return, and Tessa was grateful for her inspiration to accompany Paul home so she could thank his parents for their wedding present. She needed a distraction.

She and Paul slipped down the side steps to the front of the house. As they reached the footpath, Devil's low growl reached them from the back of Isaac's truck, but they ignored him and hurried over the strip of blue couch lawn. Above them, a silvery full moon outlined the rocky silhouette of the higher cliffs of Castle Hill, looming black and solid against the brightly lit charcoal grey sky.

She glanced at Paul walking beside her. Although not as tall as Isaac, he was a good head taller than she was, and his neat, unremarkable features had always reassured Tessa. He wasn't really as tubby as Isaac had hinted. His physique, if not stunning, was quite presentable. More importantly, Paul represented security and order. And that was what she wanted. It was only when Isaac was around that her silly mind started making comparisons and she ran into trouble. And clearly Paul found Isaac as unsettling as she did.

But now they'd almost made it through another day. Only two more to go, she told herself, and after the wedding Isaac would leave again, and she wouldn't have to worry about him any more. She would be able to concentrate on being a good wife for Paul.

It was only a short walk to Paul's house, but she wasn't surprised when he paused halfway down the street.

However, she was taken aback to see his normally placid features strained and pale and his mouth working nervously. 'So what exactly is the story between you and Isaac Masters?' he demanded.

'Story?' Tessa asked, her throat suddenly dry. 'You know very well. He's my foster brother. And he's come back for the wedding. What other story could there be?' She shivered as a wave of cold air washed over her, and she wished she'd brought something warm to slip around her shoulders. Townsville winters were mild compared with most places, but there was a decided nip in the air this evening. Or was it the chill in Paul's voice that made her so uncomfortable?

'He might be your foster brother, but you're not really related to him in any way. Your grandmother very kindly pointed that out.'

'My grandmother likes to make smart remarks,' Tessa retaliated quickly.

'I remember years ago there was a rumour going around about you two,' Paul persisted.

'So what?' cried Tessa. She chewed her upper lip desperately. 'There was a rumour about you and Melanie Whitehead, too. But I'm not making a fuss about it now.'

Paul stared at her for long, painful seconds. In the light from a street lamp, his face looked round and startled.

No, Tessa admonished herself, *he doesn't look owlish.*

'Perhaps,' he replied, 'that's because Melanie Whitehead is now married with two kids and another on the way.'

'Is she really? I had no idea, actually. Where does she live these days?'

'In Brisbane.'

'Well,' cried Tessa with a surge of triumph, 'I'm not

getting jealous of the fact that you're still keeping track of her.' Let him chew over that one.

'No, you're not, are you? I wonder why?' Paul replied very quietly, and suddenly Tessa felt that this conversation was not heading in the right direction at all.

'What are you implying now, Paul?'

'Oh, I don't know, Tess,' he sighed. 'It's just that since this guy's rocked up you've been—well, different.'

And there was no point in even trying to deny that.

'I'll admit it was a shock to see Isaac again after so long,' she said. 'It did knock me sideways at first. It was the last thing I expected. The last thing I wanted.'

'Why?'

'We—we didn't part on very good terms. We had a horrible fight.'

'Has he still got the hots for you? He's not trying to—to bother you, is he? If he is, I'll—' Paul's face puffed up with a rush of righteous fury.

'For heaven's sake, Paul! Of course not. Whatever gave you that idea?'

With a deep sigh, the hot air seemed to leave Paul just as quickly as it had arrived. He lifted his hand to the pendant at her throat. 'I don't know. I guess it was all the tear-jerker stuff about saving this precious gold and everything.'

'I didn't see anyone crying!' Tessa forced a little scoffing laugh into her voice.

But tears were exactly what she wanted to shed now. Tears for what could never be and what had to be. In the past two days the buried dreams of the last nine years—the hope that at some stage Isaac would return for her—had been dug up and exposed as useless fantasies. He hadn't come for her. He'd brought her a gift to wear on

her wedding day! This could only mean Isaac wanted her
to marry Paul.

And so she would.

'I don't think he was saving the gold particularly for
me,' she told Paul steadily. 'I think he was just hanging
on to it, like other people keep their first pay slip, and
then, when he heard I was getting married, he thought he
might as well put it to some use.' As she spoke, her words
made absolute but horrible sense. Of course Isaac hadn't
been saving his gold especially for her!

Her future lay with Paul. As if to prove that, she stood
on tiptoe and touched her lips to Paul's cool cheek. 'You
have nothing to worry about, Paul,' she whispered.

He drew her to him and pressed his lips to hers. And
even though her pulses didn't race and her heartbeat continued its usual steady rhythm, she felt better. If Paul's
kiss seemed restrained, it was probably just that they were
standing in the middle of the street in full view of any
neighbour who might chance to peek out a window. But
she felt calmer, safer. There was nothing difficult or complicated about being with Paul. It was how things were
meant to be.

By the time she walked to her house after spending a
polite half-hour chatting with Mr. and Mrs. Hammond and
then saying good-night to Paul again, allowing more
kisses on his shadowy front verandah, it seemed that her
family had gone to bed. The house was in darkness except
for a few soft table lamps left to help her find her way.
But as she walked softly down the hallway to her bedroom, she noticed a shaft of light coming from Isaac's
room. His door was not quite closed.

She paused in the dim hallway, and her hand went instantly to the heart-shaped pendant, her fingers tracing the
smooth bumps of the pearls set into the heavy gold. It was

as luxurious and beautiful to touch as it had been to look at.

Like Isaac.

His shadow briefly blocked the light, and she realised that he must be moving around in his room. Then suddenly his door opened, and he was standing before her, bare-chested, dressed only in a pair of jeans. He frowned when he saw her poised inquisitively outside his door.

'Tessa, did you want me?'

'Want you?' she asked lamely. He looked so splendidly male that her first response was to think of how desperately she wanted him.

'Want to speak to me,' he corrected, one corner of his mouth lifting ever so slightly.

'Oh, uh, yes, Isaac. I wanted to thank you for this beautiful present. I don't think I actually said anything before. It really is very, very lovely.'

Her eyes were drinking him in. The breadth of the brown shoulders, the fine shadowing of hair over the hard planes of his chest. The strength of his arms and the tapering, lean waist. She blinked. He was holding something in his hand—a book.

'I was looking through the bookshelf and I found this old diary we used to scribble in,' he said. Holding it out to her, he added, 'I was just about to take a look at it. Are you interested?'

She swallowed to relieve a sudden dryness in her throat. And her tongue flicked over her lips, which had so recently been chastely kissing Paul's. As she stood there, as if hypnotised, she composed several polite refusals in her head. Very good, sensible reasons for refusing his invitation. And then she rejected every one of them.

'Yes…yes, I'd love to.'

It was only as she drifted into his room, feeling

strangely feminine and alien amongst its overtly masculine decor, that she wondered if this was what he had
planned all along.

Just as quickly, she dismissed the foolish notion. Of
course he hadn't stayed awake, straining for the carpet-
muffled footfall that signalled her return. How could she
be so soft-headed as to even imagine such madness?

As if to contradict the wicked urging of her imagination, she sat primly on the bentwood chair by his bed with
one long leg crossed demurely over the other.

'I take it Paul's happy with you again?' he drawled.
'You gave him plenty of sweet Tessa-style reassurances
to smooth down his ruffled ego?'

She felt her eyebrows arch in surprise. Surely Isaac
wasn't jealous? 'I didn't come in here to discuss Paul.'

'Of course not,' he said quickly.

'May I?' she asked simply as she reached for the diary.

'Sure.' He tossed it to her with such easy nonchalance
that she wondered how he could carry on so calmly when
she was having difficulty with the simple task of keeping
her eyes from wandering all over him.

Tessa opened the front cover of the tattered book and
immediately felt a rush of painful nostalgia. 'Look,' she
almost sobbed, pointing a pearly fingernail to the childish
script scrawled in blue-black ink.

'Isaac Peter Masters, 45 Delaware Crescent,
Yarrawonga, Townsville, Queensland, Australia, Southern
Hemisphere, The Earth, The Universe.'

She looked up. 'Goodness,' she sighed, fighting the
urge to throw herself into his arms. 'Doesn't that take you
back? I'm sure just about every kid in the world must
write something like that at some stage.'

Isaac didn't speak, but stood watching her, his dark
features set and stern.

Nervously, she flicked over another page and couldn't help laughing as she read. *'Anyone who touches this book and who does not go by the name of Isaac Peter Masters or Theresa Rose Morrow will die a horrible death within twenty-four hours. At midnight!!!'* Laughter bubbled in her throat.

He sat on the bed, reached over and turned dog-eared pages. 'Here's an entry of mine,' he said softly. 'Read it.'

Tessa looked at him, suddenly sensitive to the fierce glint in his eyes. *'I bought Tessa a pearl necklace for her birthday.'* She paused, her throat tightening.

'Your fourteenth birthday,' Isaac said with a grim smile.

'I loved those pearls,' whispered Tessa, and she felt her lips tremble slightly.

'That was before I started part-time jobs. I bought them in a chain store. They were only cheap imitations, of course.' A raven black tumble of hair fell across his face.

'Oh, Isaac,' she whispered. 'I knew they were inexpensive, but it never mattered.' She was glad his eyes were downcast as she added, 'I've still got them, you know.'

He flicked his hair away to stare at her, eyes wide and startled. 'That cheap little string of pearls? After all this time?' He swallowed twice, his throat working rapidly, and his agitation did all kinds of damage to her self-control.

'They've broken a couple of times,' she admitted, wanting to reach out and stroke his trembling lips.

'You—you've mended them?'

'Yes. I took them to the jewellers and had them restrung properly. Of course they tried to tell me—both times—that the pearls weren't worth it.'

'Of course they weren't.'

'But, Isaac, they were to me.'

He sat silent and still, staring at her and looking thoroughly miserable. Tessa's fingers crept to the new pearls at her neck. 'These mean a great deal to me, too.'

Her words hung in the silent night for the longest time, while he seemed to fight for breath. Tessa stared at him, her heart thundering in her chest. He couldn't return her gaze. He snatched at the rough fabric of the woven bedspread.

'What else did we write in that damned book?'

She felt her mouth twist into a sad, lopsided smile as she leafed through the yellowed pages.

'December fifteenth.' she read, 'This is one of my entries. *Isaac's gone away to pick mangoes down at Bowen and I'm so bored!! He's only coming home for Christmas Day and Boxing Day. I'm stuck with Alice for the whole holidays and all she wants to do is chase boys or smoke disgusting cigarettes behind the garden shed. I tried one yesterday and I threw up. Alice just laughed.*'

'This is ancient history,' Isaac sighed.

And she suddenly had the distinct impression that he was less interested in the book than in watching her.

'Your hair gleams like polished gold in that lamplight,' he said softly, confirming her notion.

Oh, Isaac! she wanted to cry. *Touch it. Touch my hair. Touch me!*

But of course she could say no such thing. Instead she closed the book and allowed it to fall open again, and there on the page was a lock of that same hair. She looked at him with mock reproach. 'That's the hair you cut off because I was always fiddling with it.'

'So it is,' he whispered.

And she felt her mind slipping oh, so easily back to those intimate days when he'd regarded every part of her as his.

'I never minded that you cut my hair,' she whispered, not daring to make eye contact with him. If she did, there could be no disguising her longing. Nevertheless, some wicked instinct urged her to lift her hair away from her face with a suggestive gesture and to curve her lips into a smile that felt as sultry as that of any screen goddess.

Touch me, Isaac.

He reached out to caress the wing of hair. Mesmerised, she turned her face so that her lips brushed his arm. Then impulsively, she pressed them warmly into his flesh, her lips parting so that she could feel the warm, tense muscles meet the moist, inner softness of her mouth.

Love me, Isaac.

Isaac's hand cradled her chin, lifting her face. His trembling fingers traced the outline of her parted lips, and she kissed his fingertips.

'Golden girl,' he whispered. 'You are so, so beautiful.' He lowered his lips to hers, and Tessa heard a small whimper escape as his mouth joined hers.

Briefly his lips cherished her. Then he let out a strangled moan, and the kiss turned savage, his mouth taking hers with hot and eager urgency. Sharing his desperation, Tessa surrendered to his every demand. Isaac's hands moved over her with a wild exploration that knew no barriers, eagerly discovering her once more.

Her memories had been but a dim shadow of the warm, living wonder of his touch. Her whole body seemed to burst into flames as his hands traced hungrily over her. It had been far too long since she'd been in his arms.

Was this sin? Was it destiny?

There was no way she could pause to dissect the situation. No amount of self-recrimination could stop her now. Every longing she'd secretly nurtured for the past ntine years took hold, the heady, mind-numbing force of desire, the sweetness of sharing everything with Isaac.

His mouth, his lips and tongue teased then tasted and took hers with a groaning need as fierce as her own. His hands wanted to feel all of her at once. He held her hard against the thrusting force of his arousal, and she felt her flaring response swelling and filling her.

Three days, three years, three hours from now—the future could do with her whatever it willed. Her reality was now. Falling onto the bed with Isaac. Burying her face in the silky blackness of his hair and running her eager hands over his broad, firm chest.

He lifted the heart away from the base of her throat and kissed her neck and drifted kisses along her collarbone, creating blissful shudders deep inside her. In return, she raised her face and pressed her lips to the hollow above his collarbone and licked the saltiness she found there. A sigh of sheer pleasure escaped her. She trailed her mouth across his chest, following the arrowing of hair to where it disappeared beneath his jeans.

Oh, Isaac. This was her Isaac. Driven by a fresh surge of wild longing, her hand reached for the fastener at his waist.

Mistake.

His hand grabbed hers savagely and wrenched it away.

'My God, Tessa,' he panted. 'What the hell!' In one sweeping movement, he thrust her aside and leapt from the bed.

She lay in a tumbled, bewildered heap, hurting more than she could bear.

'Isaac.' Her hair had fallen across her face, and her eyes were blinded with a rush of hot, angry tears. She couldn't see his disgust, but she could hear it in his voice.

'Tessa, how could you?'

How could I help it? she wanted to cry.

'I—I don't know. Isaac, I thought...'

'What did you think?' he asked through gritted teeth while he snatched his eyes away from her exposed creamy thighs. 'That you could take a little pleasure with me during the final countdown to your wedding day?'

'No, of course not!'

The truth, she realised with a burst of sanity, was that she hadn't been thinking at all. She'd been responding with mindless instinct. It had felt for all the world as if she'd been obeying some primal law, doing what she'd been born to do.

Loving Isaac.

'You don't love him, do you?'

'Who?' she asked.

'Paul bloody Hammond. Who else?' Isaac spat the words out. The brutality of his question hit her with a force that clenched her stomach and closed around her heart. She cringed at Isaac's scowling, dark-faced abhorrence.

'Paul?' she whispered vaguely, struggling to free her mind from the memory of Isaac in her arms, Isaac's mouth on hers, Isaac's body needing her.

'The man you are going to marry on Saturday.' Isaac taunted her. 'The poor bastard. Does he know what kind of wife he's getting? Does he know how you are planning to keep your hot little body satisfied for the next thirty or forty years?'

Even as she flinched at his angry accusations, Tessa struggled to respond. But where could she begin? Isaac would never comprehend the understanding she and Paul shared. There was no way she could begin to explain her acceptance of compromise, of settling for second best.

Isaac understood nothing about her! He could not poscibly have known the desperation she felt when he left her. He had no idea how sickened she was at the thought of his going away again. But she couldn't lie here grovelling and begging this man not to leave her a second time. It wasn't worth the humiliation. If nothing else, she had gathered some pride over the past nine years.

She sat up haughtily and swept her hair from her face, tugged her skirt down from around her hips and reached with her feet for her shoes. Isaac watched in stony silence.

As she stood up, he snapped at her, 'Poor Paul may not make love to you the way you need, Queen Tess, but he does come from the right family, doesn't he?'

Startled, Tessa stared at him, her eyes round and questioning. 'I've no idea what you mean.'

A bewildered frown shadowed his face, but she was too confused, hurt and angry to care. What did it matter that they would never understand each other? The most important thing was very clear. Isaac could take her into his arms again and then, just as easily, let her go. He'd loved her and left her once already. Wouldn't she ever learn?

A toad didn't change its warts.

Tessa backed out of the room. As she paused in the doorway she said bitterly, 'How could I have ever made the mistake of loving you?'

In a final surge of desperation, she raised her hands to the clasp at the back of her neck. For a terrible moment, she thought she would not be able to get it undone, but then the two halves slipped apart. With as much aplomb as her broken spirit could resurrect, she tossed the beautiful heart to him. And without another word, she hurried down the hall to her bedroom.

CHAPTER SIX

Two days to go...

This morning Isaac would leave. Tessa was sure of that.

Last night, when she'd flung the golden heart at him while her own heart pounded in her chest fit to burst, she'd hoped that he would go straight away.

How could she face him again? Even if Isaac still felt attracted to her, what good was that? It couldn't change anything now. In his arms last night, there'd been no talk of love, only a desperate, brief meeting of two bodies. And physical need was such a basic instinct. It had nothing to do with the finer qualities necessary for a lasting relationship—qualities like love and trust and compatibility.

How could you? he'd cried at her. And she cringed at the reminder that their interlude in his room had all been her fault. A wave of self-disgust hit her in the stomach. For pity's sake! She'd panted and lusted after Isaac with all the control of an alley cat in heat.

But a small, persistent thought nagged at her. Perhaps he *had* waited up deliberately. After all, the invitation to look at the diary was about as subtle as the old line, 'Come and see my etchings, my dear.' Maybe he'd laid a trap for her and she'd fallen for it. But why, then, when she responded with the kind of impulsive honesty she'd always offered Isaac, had he shoved her off with a curse?

She sat at her window, watching the still waters of Cleveland Bay pick up the tiny grey shimmers of early morning light, and tried to reassure herself that she was almost certainly better off with a safe and steady husband like Paul Hammond. Someone who came from a stable family background and who had complete confidence in his ability to be a supportive family man.

And didn't she wear Paul's ring as a symbol of her promise to marry him? She couldn't possibly contemplate standing him up at the altar.

Tessa dropped her throbbing head into her hands. This situation was terrible. If only Isaac had never returned!

It was mildly comforting to realise that her heartless ingratitude last night had probably performed the kind of ruthless surgery she and Isaac needed. Her rejection of his beautiful gift should have effectively severed any remaining trace of Isaac's feelings for her. Cut him free.

Free to leave.

She went to breakfast early, expecting to find him gone. But there he was, calmly helping himself to coffee. Tessa considered fleeing. There was no way she could face an early morning sparring match.

But on the surface, everything appeared normal. Rosalind had set the table on the deck with a bright floral cloth, a huge bowl of tropical fruit and jaunty yellow crockery. Beyond the cheery table setting, the tropical winter sun highlighted the sparkling water of the bay and splashed light over the colourful hillside. The aroma of coffee wafted on the still morning air.

'Good morning,' Tessa said as breezily as she could.

Isaac nodded coldly, and Tessa willed her treacherous cheeks not to blush.

Rosalind said, 'Good morning, dear,' with undisguised impatience and then turned to Isaac. 'You're just the man I need,' she said, and flashed a brighter smile at him than Tessa had seen from her mother since he arrived. Then Rosalind's mouth drooped into a definite pout. 'The odd-job man I was relying on to help me transport everything to the marquee over the next couple of days has hurt his back.'

She managed to make it sound as if the man had deliberately had an accident just to inconvenience her.

Isaac lowered himself into a navy canvas director's chair and spoke firmly. 'I'm sorry, Rosalind, if you're hoping that I can help you, I don't think—'

'Isaac,' Rosalind interrupted, her voice suddenly as cold and sharp as a bayonet. 'You can't let me down. You've come back now and upset Tessa's wedding plans.'

'Nothing's been upset, Mum.' Tessa broke in, suddenly willing to overlook the minor detail that she'd spent an entire night feeling unspeakably miserable.

Isaac stared at her in stony silence.

'I'm glad to hear that, darling,' replied Rosalind. 'But Isaac understands what I mean. The least he can do for us now is help ensure you have a lovely wedding.'

Tessa gulped.

'I was actually thinking it might be best if I leave,' Isaac said quietly, his eyes fixed on the coffee cup he was filling.

Tessa felt a stab of dismay. How ridiculous! Wasn't this exactly what she wanted? She heard the sharp intake of Rosalind's breath.

'Forgive me, Rosalind,' he continued, then paused, and his eyes flickered warily over Tessa before he took a sip of coffee. 'As I remember it, the last time I did you a favour for Tessa's sake was nine years ago. I certainly didn't agree with you then, as you well know.'

'*My* sake? Isaac, What on earth—'

'That's enough, Isaac!' Rosalind interrupted. Her pale cheeks flamed bright red, and she glared at him.

It was nowhere near enough! Tessa's mind whirled with a million questions. 'Mum, tell me. What's this about?'

But Rosalind and Isaac ignored her. They glared at each other.

'Isaac,' Tessa persisted, desperate to understand. 'You're not telling me you went away for *my* sake?'

At last Isaac seemed to hear her. He looked at her bleakly, and for a moment seemed at a loss for words. His mouth opened and shut. Then he shook his head. 'Your sake, my sake. It was better for everyone. But let's not go into all that now,' he hurriedly added before she could interrupt. 'Rosalind, if I leave now, it would once again be for the best.'

Rosalind's complexion paled under her carefully applied make-up. Tessa could almost see her mother's mind whirring, deciding her best response. The set of her fine jaw hardened, and she eyed Isaac shrewdly over the rim of her cup.

'Yesterday I might have agreed with you,' she said. 'Poor Paul felt totally upstaged by your flamboyant gift.'

If only she knew what had happened to that gift, Tessa thought grimly, Rosalind might not have looked so pained. In fact, if she had seen her daughter tossing it at Isaac, she'd have been positively jubilant.

But with any luck her mother would never know about last night.

'Now, with my handyman out of action,' Rosalind continued, 'I just haven't time to find someone else suitable to help with all the preparations. Believe me, I would if I could.'

'Oh, I believe you, Rosalind.' Isaac shot her a sardonic grin as he bit into a slice of rockmelon.

'I need someone I can—trust,' Rosalind said a trifle awkwardly. 'I don't have time to check out another man's credentials and background properly. If I ring an agency they could send me absolutely anyone at all.'

'Someone they found on the streets?' Isaac asked, his mouth twisted in a bitter grimace.

Rosalind glared at him as she set her coffee cup carefully on its saucer. 'We don't have time for your cryptic style of humour,' she replied, gathering her composure with a distinct straightening of her shoulders and a lift of her chin. 'This is a day for action. And as far as I'm concerned, Tessa's wedding now depends very much on your willingness to cooperate, Isaac.'

An experienced tactician, Rosalind didn't wait for Isaac's response. She stood hastily, glanced at her watch and spoke quickly. 'Now I must dash to the florists. You should be able to help yourselves to breakfast. My daily help, Mrs. Pierce, will deal with any problems in the kitchen. I'll be back around ten, so after you've dropped Tessa at work, don't go anywhere, Isaac. That's when I'll need you.' Then Rosalind swept off the deck and disappeared into the house.

Isaac glared after her before scowling at Tessa. In what appeared to be a fit of disgust, he snapped his hand to his forehead in an angry imitation of a military salute.

'You don't have to—' Tessa began.

'I know I don't *have* to do anything!' Isaac barked, but then his face relaxed into a rueful smile. He slanted his slow, mocking gaze in her direction. 'But it isn't every day I get to rescue your wedding single-handed.'

Tessa tried to feign a careless laugh, but all that emerged was a rather shaky bleat.

'So,' said Isaac, leaning back in his chair with an exaggeratedly casual sprawl. 'My day's organised. How about yours?'

Tessa blinked. His interest was unexpected. 'It's the last

day of term,' she told him. 'I always try to plan something
fun for the children so that they at least start their holidays
happily.'

'Their holidays are pretty rough?'

'Yes.' Tessa sighed. 'Most of the children go home to
less than ideal conditions. Some go hungry, others are
abused. Almost all are neglected in one way or another.'

Isaac shook his head slowly while he stared at Tessa
with a dark, thoughtful gaze. 'So what's the treat for today?' he asked quietly.

'I try to give them simple fun. Lavishing short bursts
of luxury on them doesn't help much. So today we're
having a treasure hunt. I hide little surprises—just simple,
natural treasures that I've collected. Things like those
wonderful chocolate brown seedpods from Moreton Bay
chestnuts, or beautiful shells, pine cones painted silver,
water-worn pebbles all smooth and perfectly round—that
sort of thing.' She paused and eyed Isaac with challenging
directness. 'The sorts of things you used to love when you
were a boy.'

His bleak expression shocked her.

'I'm sorry, Isaac. I didn't mean to bring back bad memories. I know you had a terrible time when you were little.
But I learnt a lot about dealing with these children from
living—with you.'

His eyes, dark and sombre, stared dazedly at a point
past her shoulder. Then with a shake of his head, he
blinked and focused.

'A treasure hunt sounds great,' he said. 'I hope you
have a great day.'

'Thanks. We'd better be going.' She jumped to her feet.
'I have to hide all the treasure before the children arrive.'

'You haven't eaten anything again.'

'Haven't I?' Her nerves were stretched so tautly she

could hardly remember how to place one foot after the other let alone whether she'd eaten.

Isaac picked out a rosy apple from the fruit bowl and tossed it to her. 'An apple for the teacher,' he drawled. And as she walked away to collect her things, he called after her, 'Now don't forget to eat it.'

Thank heavens she'd managed to keep herself busy for the rest of the day, Tessa thought that afternoon as she watched her preschoolers' eager delight in the treasure hunt. She'd been distracted by a very disturbing phone call earlier in the day from the city council's social services department. It seemed the takeover bid to buy up a great deal of property in the area, including the land on which the preschool stood, was about to succeed. But apparently there had been some allegations of shady dealing. Evidence was emerging in a court hearing that showed a lot of South Townsville properties were involved in some sort of scam.

As things stood, Tessa had no idea whether the preschool would still exist when she returned from her honeymoon. Her gaze travelled over the bare strip of yard at the back of the centre. It might be ugly and dilapidated, but it echoed with delighted squeals and laughter. It wrenched at her heart to think that these children might be about to lose their little sanctuary of happiness and safety.

'Miss Tessa, Miss Tessa, I've found one! I've found some treasure!' Gregory came running towards her with his treasure, a beautiful pearly, pink and white shell, carefully cradled in his hands. 'I found it buried in the sandpit!' he cried excitedly.

'It's beautiful, Gregory.' Tessa laughed and ruffled his curling red hair before he darted away again.

The cool afternoon breeze rising off nearby Ross River wafted pleasantly over the yard. She wriggled her shoulders, trying to release the tight knots of tension. This was the first time she'd had a moment to herself for hours, but of course the minute she took time out, unwanted thoughts claimed her attention.

She had dreamed some fanciful dreams over the past nine years, and now they lay in the dust around her. Tessa knew with absolute certainty that all her foolish notions about Isaac coming back with loving, open arms amounted to no more than a grand case of self-delusion. She was grateful for that timely revelation.

But she did regret throwing back his beautiful gift.

A keepsake, Lydia had called it. What a lovely name that was. Perhaps it would have been cheering in the years to come to be able to take the locket out from time to time to look at it, to treasure the memories it represented. As she watched the children's delight over their finds, she reflected that to have a little treasure buried away helped people get through the everyday ordinariness of their lives.

Even though Isaac no longer wanted her, and in spite of the fact that they would never again be lovers, she could have kept the heart as a precious reminder of the kind of loving she had only ever experienced with him.

Her eyes misted, and she searched the pocket of her slacks for a tissue. She was being maudlin and sentimental. But the heart *was* made from gold Isaac had carried with him all these years, while she'd been trying to imagine where he was and what he was doing. *And* he'd added the pearls—to remind her of his first gift!! That had to be a Byronic gesture, whatever way she looked at it. And she had thrown it back in his face. She would never have the golden heart now.

She was blowing her nose rather loudly when she heard Hilda's voice behind her.

'They're all outside hunting for treasure at the moment.'

It seemed they had a guest. Perhaps one of the parents had arrived to pick up a child early. She turned and smiled in greeting. The smile dissolved.

Behind Hilda strode Isaac, tall, dark and looking slightly uncertain.

'This seems to be a big success,' he said as he reached her and noted the happy children swarming in the yard.

She was glad she'd been leaning against the doorjamb and could clutch it for support. 'Isaac? What on earth are you doing here? Aren't you supposed to be flat out, working for Mum?' she queried weakly.

'All done.' He grinned. 'Rosalind's just overanxious. There wasn't really all that much to do. So I brought you some light entertainment.' His gaze dropped to his feet.

Tessa's startled eyes found Devil squatting quietly at his master's heel. 'You shouldn't bring the dog in here,' she said nervously. 'I'm sure there's something in the lease about animals on the premises.'

'You have three pet turtles in a tank. I met Hop, Step and Jump last time I was here.'

'For heaven's sake, Isaac. I thought you were more observant. There are major biological differences between a penny turtle and a cattle dog. Your Devil will frighten the children.'

'No, he won't,' answered Isaac confidently. 'Cattle dogs love kids. Has the treasure hunt more or less finished?'

When she nodded, he responded with another grin. 'Just watch this, Miss Tessa.'

'But, Isaac!'

She was angry, breathless, intrigued...

Ignoring her, Isaac strode into the centre of the yard, and Devil trotted obediently behind him. Some of the children paused and stared. At a quiet word from Isaac, Devil sat and held out a paw. Danny, a cheeky Aboriginal boy, edged forward.

'He wants to shake hands,' Isaac told the boy.

'Okay.' Danny grinned boldly. He took the dog's paw and shook it. Other children clustered around, chattering excitedly.

'My turn!'

'Can I shake his hand, too?'

Soon everyone was joining in. Tessa felt a small hand slip into hers. She looked down. 'Rosie, are you frightened of the dog?'

The little girl nodded and looked at Tessa, round, dark eyes peering out of her brown face.

'You can stay here with me,' reassured Tessa, and she felt a slight smugness that her prediction about the dog had been at least partially correct.

Nevertheless, Tessa watched with bemusement as Isaac and Devil entertained the rest of her brood. Wary at first, in case the dog suddenly snapped at a small limb, she gradually relaxed. Devil obeyed every quiet command of Isaac's instantly. She couldn't help but be mollified by the children's happy excitement. The dog shook hands patiently with the entire giggling group.

When they were almost finished, Isaac noticed Rosie nestling shyly against Tessa. He crossed to them and squatted down eye to eye with the little girl. 'Hello,' he said.

Rosie snuggled more closely against Tessa's legs. Tessa hoped Isaac wasn't about to force the frightened child to make contact with the dog.

'I was wondering if you could help me?' he asked Rosie.

The girl remained silent, fixing Isaac with a steady brown-eyed gaze.

'I was wondering if you know where the balls are kept. I need some balls for Devil's next trick.'

Slowly the little girl nodded.

'That's great!' Isaac beamed at her. He held out his hand. 'Can you show me?'

The little hand left Tessa's and took Isaac's without hesitation. She led him to a toy box.

'Can you throw the ball for the puppy?' Isaac asked when they were outside again.

Rosie giggled. 'Yes,' she said, and tossed the ball. The next minute she was clutching Isaac's hand and squealing with as much terror and delight as the other children when Devil leapt into the air and caught the ball. Tessa could not suppress a sudden surge of admiration for the skilful way he'd charmed Rosie.

It seemed the dog could do no end of clever tricks. He caught the balls and Frisbees the children tossed, performed astonishing back flips, hopped around on his hind legs and then, when he finally flopped exhausted at his master's feet, he tolerated the children's patting and hugging and even climbing onto him.

And Isaac joked and chatted to the children as easily as if he were a well-known and favourite uncle. But what surprised Tessa even more was that he genuinely seemed to like the children!

He flashed her an elated smile that tripped her heartbeat. Then he called to them all, 'Who's hungry?'

'They've already had their—' Tessa began, but her protest was drowned out by a predictable chorus of eager replies.

'Me! Me!'

'I'm starving!'

'I'll be right back,' Isaac promised. And he was as good as his word, returning quickly and carrying a large Esky. He tossed the lid back and revealed a tempting assortment of ice-creams.

'Line up, then, and you can take your pick.' He looked at Tessa, his mouth twitching. 'One little treat won't hurt them.'

'No, of course not,' she replied. *But it's hurting me!* She wanted to cry. *Stay aloof, stay angry, Isaac. Don't let me see this side of you now.*

Stay away!

He came and stood beside her. 'They're great kids, aren't they?'

'They certainly are.'

His mouth curved in a faintly penitent smile. 'I hope it wasn't too intrusive of me to turn up like this.'

'It was obviously a welcome intrusion,' Tessa replied politely, indicating with a sweeping gesture the throng of happy faces, tongues eagerly licking ice-creams. 'When on earth did you have time to teach your dog all those tricks?'

Isaac shrugged. 'There's not much entertainment out on the mining sites. You find yourself doing all sorts of things to fill in the hours.'

Tessa shivered at the thought of Isaac alone and possibly lonely with only a dog for company.

'You're doing a great job here, Tess.' The unfathomable dark eyes held her for moment. He put one hand to her cheek, and it took every ounce of her strength to hold still. 'I hope you can sweet-talk Paul into letting you stay on working here.'

'He's a bit of a pushover really,' she said with a jaunty

confidence she was far from feeling. For a fleeting moment, she considered telling him about the takeover threat and the court case, but just as quickly dismissed the notion. It would be foolish to involve Isaac in her affairs.

His eyebrow rose in a questioning arch. 'I hope you can win your husband over,' he replied quietly. 'Now can I help you clean up?'

'You most certainly can,' Tessa said quickly, trying to ignore the unhealthy dive her heart had taken when Isaac spoke of her *husband*. 'There are drips of ice-cream everywhere.' Then, as she looked around the room, she cried with disbelief, 'Oh, no, Rosie! Don't feed your ice-cream to Devil!' She shook her head at Isaac and couldn't help smiling. 'I'll admit you've won a convert there.'

He grinned at her, a warm, heart-stopping smile that rippled right through her to her very toes.

Tessa was grateful for the diversion of mopping up. She'd trained the children well, and soon they were working in little teams, putting the preschool to rights for the holidays. Isaac worked alongside them cheerfully.

'How about you check the yard for overlooked treasure,' he suggested to Tessa, glancing over his shoulder as he hunkered down next to a little girl called Elsie who was carefully wiping a tabletop.

Whose show is this? Tessa wanted to demand. But she was glad to escape from the disturbing sight of Isaac playing the role of the charming charity man. Why couldn't he stick to being obnoxious? It was much easier to hate him then!

She slipped into the playground, raked the sandpit and checked the pot plants. It seemed every last treasure had been claimed. After slowly circling the yard she was about to return inside when she saw something white caught between two dilapidated fence palings. She hadn't rememhered putting a shell there. But it wasn't a shell she discovered as she crossed the yard. It was a very familiar small, flat, rectangular box.

And inside was a heart-shaped pendant studded with pearls.

She stood in the middle of the yard holding it, tears streaming down her face. Oh, why had Isaac done this? Did this mean he understood? He cared? One thing was certain. He was messing her up—one hundred per cent! She stood trembling and fighting more tears, and it was a long time before she was able to go inside the building.

And to her relief, by then Isaac and Devil had gone.

At least, she told herself with a painful sigh, she should be able to get through the evening without having to face him again. She badly needed breathing space to be able to focus on Paul and her future. And there was no reason for Isaac to turn up at the wedding rehearsal.

So why, Tessa found herself asking later that evening, as she stood on the steps of St. James' Cathedral, was Isaac's black truck, complete with dog cage, pulling into the cathedral parking lot?

Damn and blast the man! Just when she needed to put him right out of her mind, he turned up to haunt and agitate her. Last night they'd been practically clawing and spitting at each other. This afternoon she'd seen another side of him that had completely destroyed all her well-developed opinions. And now, heaven help her, she felt again the familiar tug of longing that the briefest glimpse of Isaac evoked.

Where was Paul when she needed him?

Nigel Rivers, the tall, sandy-headed best man, was also a colleague of Paul's, and he had arrived at her house with some weak explanation about Paul being held up at court. Tessa swallowed the knot of anxiety tightening her throat.

As Isaac's vehicle made its final turn into a parking bay, Tessa caught sight of someone else. Surely that was her bridesmaid's merry face, red suit lapels and dark, curly hair?

'That's strange. It looks as if Isaac has brought Alice,' she said to Nigel and the dean of the cathedral. 'I can't imagine why he would need to.'

She was distinctly annoyed by the way tension tightened her stomach even more painfully. Why on earth would Alice suddenly need a lift? And from Isaac, of all people? Alice was proud of her sporty little red sedan. Apart from that, she was a very successful television journalist and a fiercely independent young woman. Paul had even gone so far as to confide to Tessa that he found her best friend a tad too feminist.

But there was nothing feminist about the way Alice was tossing her long, dark curls over one cherry-red, padded shoulder. Or the unnecessary way her short, tight, red skirt revealed almost the entire length of her sheer black tights as she negotiated the high step from Isaac's truck. Tessa had travelled in that truck, and she was quite certain that Alice didn't really need Isaac's gallantly proffered hand as she descended, or to look so gratefully at him from under her sinfully long eyelashes as if he had just rescued her from a blazing inferno.

At least Isaac dropped her hand as they crossed the bitumen drive to reach the foot of the cathedral steps, but his all too handsome face continued to wear the smug smile of a punter whose horse had come in on long odds. Added to that, he was wearing a superbly cut dark grey suit, white shirt and black silk tie, all of which enhanced his physique to an indecent level of perfection. No wonder Alice was drooling.

It didn't bother Tessa, of course, that since getting out of his vehicle, Isaac's eyes hadn't once met hers.

'Hello, young lover,' Alice called to Tessa with her usual mischievous grin. 'Feeling scared stiff about the approaching nuptials?' She shot an encouraging wink at Tessa. But somehow Tessa didn't feel encouraged. Alice was her best friend and Tessa had always loved her dearly—until now.

'Not at all,' she replied stiffly. 'Have you met the dean, Reverend Joseph, and Paul's best man, Nigel Rivers?' she continued nervously.

'Yes, we've met before,' Alice said as she dazzled the men with one of the smiles that had made her famous on camera.

'Pleased to meet you,' murmured Isaac politely, taking the other men's hands and flashing them swift smiles of greeting.

Everyone is so busy grinning at each other, Tessa thought as she stretched her lips into something she hoped resembled a smile.

Isaac's dark gaze rested briefly on her. 'Evening, Tessa.'

Her mouth froze mid-smile. 'Good evening, Isaac.'

'Paul's been held up in a rather complicated court case. Can't be helped, but he's pretty miffed,' explained Nigel.

'Bad luck,' offered Isaac, and Tessa wondered if her ears were deceiving her. His words dripped with sincerity.

'So, let's go inside.' The dean led the little group up the sandstone steps to the massive, carved wooden doors.

'It's only a small wedding party. Tessa just wanted the one attendant,' Nigel explained to Isaac. 'I take it you already know Alice, her best friend.'

'Yes, of course,' Isaac responded, allowing a spectacular smile to ripple over Alice. 'Alice and I go back a long way.'

Since when? Tessa clenched her teeth tightly to stop herself from voicing the question. Alice had been her closest girl friend since the third grade, so of course Isaac knew her, but there'd never been any special friendship between them.

A picture of Alice as a teenager flashed into her mind. She'd had five brothers and had been quite a tomboy as well as an incredibly skinny kid with freckles and braces. And she had always tried to tame her frizzy hair by plastering it down with a dozen or so bobby pins.

The picture was about as different from the curvy, long-limbed woman before them as the original ugly duckling had been from the graceful swan. A fortune at the hairdressers had transformed Alice's frizz into very fashionable Renaissance ringlets, and her smile, thanks to her orthodontist, had earned her considerable status as the region's favourite television news personality.

Men trailed after her constantly, but she laughingly discarded them all after a few dates. 'I'll try but I won't buy,' she'd told Tessa more than once. 'I don't think I could ever stay interested in just one man.'

This wasn't the first time Tessa wished she could take relationships with men as lightly.

As the party moved through the cathedral doors, the dean collected a little pile of prayer books from a table just inside and handed them out. Tessa looked at the red-carpeted aisle, the softly glowing timber pews and the gleaming brass and copper urns and crosses and took a deep breath. She had always loved churches, and this church in particular usually infused her with a sense of calm and inner peace. Her eyes wandered to the arched windows and the soaring vaulted ceilings.

She certainly needed bucket loads of inner peace now, she thought, as she darted a sideways glance at Isaac, who was striding calmly into the church beside Alice. What was he doing here? He had no right! There was no way she could practise going through the ceremony with his black eyes taking in every nuance, listening to every syllable, unnerving her beyond belief!

Tessa paused en route to the front of the church and turned to him.

'Isaac, surely you don't want to stay.' She hated the note of pleading that crept into her voice. 'You'll find this awfully boring. We—when Paul gets here, he and I could easily take Alice home.'

'Not on your life,' interjected Alice. Then she reached over and gave Tessa's arm a friendly squeeze before tucking her other arm through Isaac's. 'No offence, darling, but Isaac's taking me out to dinner straight after this.'

CHAPTER SEVEN

THE sick feeling in Tessa's stomach was *not* jealousy.

Of course Isaac had every right to take Alice out to dinner. Yet, in spite of her resolve to remain indifferent, annoying questions kept jumping into Tessa's head. How and when had Isaac met Alice? What not so subtle moves had Alice made to wangle the invitation? Most importantly, why was Isaac suddenly motivated to date her best friend and bridesmaid?

Tessa's mind whirred endlessly while the group stood at the chancel steps waiting for Paul, chatting politely with the dean about the weather and other ceremonies he'd conducted.

No, she was definitely not jealous. This hideous tension, this inability to breathe was just nerves, she told herself, and it was perfectly normal to feel on the edge of panic at a wedding rehearsal. From what she'd heard, nearly everybody got nervous at the ceremony itself, so why not for the rehearsal, as well?

But she might have felt better if she had been quite sure it was Paul's absence and not Isaac's presence that was causing her so much distress.

Eventually, the group ran out of topics for idle chitchat, and the dean started to sneak surreptitious glances at his watch. Nigel, sensing the restlessness, cleared his throat. 'Look, I hate to say it, but there is a chance Paul may be kept really late. This case he's defending…took a rather unexpected turn today.' He looked distinctly uncomfortable.

107

'Perhaps we'd better run through the service anyhow,' suggested the dean. 'Tessa, dear, you can go over the important details with your groom some time before the ceremony, can't you?'

'Of course,' she said, her voice a croak. She swallowed hard to ease the spasm in her throat.

'Now,' the dean began, peering at the group over the top of his gold-rimmed spectacles. 'We start with the bride.' He nodded an encouraging smile at Tessa, and she hoped her answering smile looked better than it felt. 'You stand in front of me here, my dear. And then the best man is next to where the groom would be, bridesmaid this side—that's right, lovely.' He looked at Isaac expectantly.

'Oh, I'm just part of the congregation,' Isaac grinned, raising his hands in a gesture of non-involvement and backing towards a front pew.

'Don't rush away. We can use you,' the dean called, his small, grey eyes brightening behind his spectacles. 'Could you stand in as our groom for now?'

'Oh, no!' cried Tessa.

And everybody looked at her curiously.

Tessa bent her head. Too bad if they thought her odd. This twist of fate was just too cruel. Tears of anger, tears of utter helplessness stung her eyes. Once again she was living her worst nightmare, only this time events had outstripped even the most bizarre scenarios conjured by her wretched imagination. This was agony. Silently she pleaded to Isaac. *I can't bear this. Please refuse. It's not necessary.*

Isaac seemed to be having difficulty answering the dean's request. 'What would I have to do?' he asked at last.

'Basically just stand here and fill in the empty space.'

The dean gave a little shrug. 'It helps everyone to get the right sense of spacing and position.'

Tessa held her breath. Her cheeks grew hot, and she felt her heart pound in her chest. Isaac looked at her, his eyes boring into her, full of black heat.

The silence that had fallen on the group was reaching the awkward stage.

'Hey, Isaac, this is only practice,' cajoled Alice with a quiet laugh. 'You sound like it's your future at stake, or something.'

Isaac's glance bounced from Tessa to Alice, and he flashed a strained smile. 'Yes, of course I'll help out,' he replied quickly.

'You won't find yourself accidentally married to the wrong person.' The dean chuckled as if anxious to cover any awkwardness. 'I've never been known to make that mistake yet,' he continued, enjoying his own little joke. 'Although,' he added with a heartfelt sigh, and Tessa wondered why on earth he chose to look straight at her as he spoke, 'I'm afraid there are far too many couples who discover too late they have made the wrong choice.'

Another silence fell, then Isaac stepped forward and stood beside Tessa. 'I'll try anything once.' He looked at her with an embarrassed, lopsided smile.

'I promise I won't be pronouncing anybody husband and wife until Saturday,' the dean continued his joke, and Tessa wanted to scream at him.

Just get this over with! Please! She would go mad if she allowed herself to think about the tremble in Isaac's voice as he questioned the need to replace Paul.

Perhaps the dean sensed her urgency for he addressed them all with a marked squaring of his shoulders. 'I will start the ceremony, once Tessa and Paul are in place here, by announcing, we have come together in the sight of God for the joining in marriage of this man Paul and this woman Theresa.'

Even if I don't feel calm, I must look calm, Tessa told herself.

For a fleeting, foolish second as Isaac took his place beside her, an image had flashed into her mind of herself standing at the altar in her wedding gown. Looking up, she'd smiled through the filmy haze of Lydia's heirloom veil at Isaac. He was standing erect and handsome beside her and was gazing at her, his dark eyes shining with admiration and love.

Idiot! She darted a hand across her eyes to banish the ridiculous mirage. The days of childish fantasy were long gone. She was right in the middle of very serious, adult-style reality!! As the dean continued to outline the service, she stifled further foolishness by concentrating on her surroundings. First she examined the delicate crocheted lace edges of the white altar cloth. From there her eyes wandered upwards to examine each pane of richly coloured glass in the rose window set high in the brick wall behind the altar.

Isaac was standing stiffly beside her, and she didn't dare glance at his face. He seemed to be concentrating very carefully on what the dean was saying.

'After that, I will go on to tell everybody how marriage is a symbol of God's love for us and how it must not be entered into lightly or carelessly.'

Tessa sensed Isaac turning slightly towards her, but she kept her eyes straight ahead. There'd been nothing light or careless in her decision to marry Paul. So why did she feel so light-headed now? She had the horrible feeling that at any moment she might burst into tears or just as easily into a fit of giggles. Did this mean she was hysterical?

She bit her lip hard. The dean read out the vows that

Paul would make, and as she listened, Tessa forced herself to think about Paul's reliability and steadiness and how lucky she was to be gaining such a dependable husband.

'Now, for the bride's vows.' The dean smiled. 'My dear, repeat after me…I, Theresa Rose, in the presence of God…'

Tessa swallowed deeply and hoped her dry throat would obey her better than her pounding heart and shaking knees. 'I, Theresa Rose, in the presence of God…'

'Take you, Paul Francis, to be my husband…'

With the worst sense of timing, Tessa happened to glance into Isaac's face at that moment. The ferocity of his expression stunned her. She opened her mouth to repeat the words, but no sound emerged. For long seconds she seemed frozen, staring at Isaac and unable to speak. If only he didn't look so fierce she would be able to go ahead.

At her prolonged silence, Isaac's eyes narrowed, his gaze still fixed on hers. Eventually, he must have understood something of her panic, because his expression softened slightly. The tiniest of smiles lifted the corners of his mouth, even though his eyes remained fierce.

'Go on,' he whispered, his breath warm on her forehead. She felt his hand reach for hers, and his fingers squeezed hers gently. And it took every ounce of her willpower to banish memories of how those fingers had caressed and explored, tantalised and tempted her the evening before.

She breathed in deeply. 'Take you, P-Paul Francis, to be my husband,' she managed to say at last.

'I'm afraid you will need to be a little louder, Tessa,' said the dean gently. 'To have and to hold.'

'To have and to hold.'

'That's better. From this day forward.'

'From this day forward.'

Somehow, she did it. *For better for worse, for richer for poorer, in sickness and in health, to love and to cherish, as long as we both shall live.* The words fell from her lips automatically. It was almost like reciting a multiplication table, only much, much harder. She had never felt so miserable.

Not even when Isaac had left her.

She knew that each word she spoke was leading her away from Isaac and into Paul's arms, and yet strangely, it was the warmth of Isaac's hand holding hers that kept her going.

'And now, of course, the best man must hand me the ring,' the dean said to Nigel.

Loud footsteps sounded on the sandstone floor. Tessa swung round to see Paul, looking flustered and very put out, hurrying towards them through a side chapel. His light brown hair was all awry, as if he had run his hands through it many times.

'Ah,' cried the dean with delight. 'We have a bridegroom. Welcome, my dear fellow, you're just in time to practise the giving of the ring.'

Paul rushed up to them looking flushed and angry. He glared at the dean. 'Why have you started without me? I sent a message. I would have been here if I could, but I—I wasn't in a position to try to persuade the judge to adjourn.' He swung sharply to confront Isaac, who was standing in his place next to Tessa. 'What—what the hell's going on, Masters?' His round face darkened to an unattractive shade of salmon pink.

'Steady on,' Isaac murmured, 'the lady is all yours.' A deep sweep of his arm and a cynical lift of one dark eyebrow accompanied his words. 'I was only the part-time fill-in.'

Paul eyed Isaac suspiciously before he took his place beside Tessa. She set her hand on his. 'We didn't think you'd mind our starting. I hope you haven't had too dreadful a day,' she said to him.

He scowled at her for several seconds. 'It's been quite a bunfight,' he muttered, still looking florid and quite stressed. Then his features relaxed into a weak smile. 'Ah, well, this makes up for it,' he said and planted a wet kiss on her cheek.

'I'll catch a breath of fresh air,' muttered Isaac and strode away down the long aisle.

Paul delivered his lines clearly and loudly, if a little pompously, and Tessa was able to respond with equal calm and clarity until she came to the final line, *May God enable us to grow in love together.*

It was then that she found herself praying silently. *Yes, God, that is exactly what I need. Please help my love for Paul to grow and grow.* But as she prayed, her cheeks grew hot and her stomach squirmed guiltily. She didn't add, *Until I love him as much as I love Isaac,* but the words were there in her heart.

And wasn't God supposed to know what secrets lay in her heart?

To her relief, the rehearsal was over shortly after that, and the group made its way to the cathedral's west door. Isaac lounged against a column just inside the entrance.

'You came through clear as a bell,' he drawled as Tessa approached.

She chose not to respond, but her confusion ensured her cheeks remained scarlet until Alice's voice penetrated her wild thoughts.

'I'm positively starving,' Alice announced, and her eyes were fixed on Isaac. She kept her eyes feasting on him as she leant over to Tessa and whispered, 'Yum—

I'm thinking about dessert already,' Then she sauntered up to Isaac, her bottom wriggling in the short, tight skirt, and pouted. 'Feed me, man.'

Isaac's black gaze flickered over Alice with undisguised amusement. 'With pleasure,' he responded. Pushing away from the column, he straightened and offered Alice an arm, which she took eagerly. 'We'll depart then,' he said.

There was no doubt, Tessa noted with a spurt of irritation, that Isaac's whole manner expressed relief mingled with relaxed expectation.

'I'll see you on the big day, Tess,' Alice called over her shoulder as she and Isaac moved off arm in arm.

Tessa kept her smile in place for the entire time they took to laugh and joke their way down the cathedral steps before disappearing into the dark cavern of the unlit car park. But if she had been holding on to her smile for her fiancé's sake, she might have saved her energy, for Paul's attention was concentrated elsewhere. In muttered undertones, he and Nigel were deeply involved in a fierce discussion of the day's case.

She had never felt more alone.

CHAPTER EIGHT

ONLY one more day to go...

The second last night before her wedding seemed endless. Tessa spent it tossing and turning, her mind tussling unproductively with her dilemma. But at last it was morning. She peered out her bedroom window, taking in the clear blue skies and crisp winter sunshine. It was a beautiful day, and there was every indication that tomorrow would be just as lovely. Despite the invigorating weather, Tessa felt drained, tired and numb.

She dressed and wandered down to breakfast, going through the motions of eating a little, sipping coffee and inhaling the delicate hint of jasmine that drifted from the garden below. Only when she allowed her mind to replay the image of Isaac disappearing into the night with Alice clinging to him like a leech were her feelings stirred. And that was a pointless exercise. She sighed.

She shouldn't be upset with Alice. As far as her friend was concerned, she had a green light to chase full steam ahead after Isaac. He was, in her terminology, a HUM— a hot, unattached male. End of story.

Of course Alice had known how Tessa felt about Isaac back in the dim, distant past of their university years. But after some time, Tessa had managed to convince her friend, along with everyone else in her circle, that she had recovered from the affair.

'I'm over Isaac,' she had schooled herself to say. And she'd made the words leave her lips with exactly the right blend of carelessness and conviction, so that people im-

mediately believed her. After a while Isaac's name never
entered conversations. Eventually her family and friends,
including Alice, assumed he'd faded into that forgotten
collection of boyfriends every girl discards as she em-
braces adulthood.

And Isaac had never given Tessa any indication that his
feelings had changed since his angry rejection of her when
he walked out of this house and clear out of her life nine
years ago. She hadn't asked him about other women, but
of course there would have been hundreds. The passionate
kisses they'd exchanged the other night meant nothing to
him. Any normal male would have responded with similar
enthusiasm if a woman had entered his bedroom and come
on to him as she had. No wonder he was disgusted! And
small wonder he wanted to make his situation crystal clear
to her by dating someone else!

Actions spoke louder than words.

It was bewildering how her mind could unravel with
surprising dexterity all the complexities of her one-way
relationship with Isaac, but when she contemplated her
marriage to Paul, just twenty-four hours away, her thinking grew sluggish. She knew her feelings about this wedding were not as they should be, but she couldn't quite
put her finger on the problem.

It wasn't Paul. He was admirable husband material—
upright, wealthy, stable and generous. She hadn't been
pressured into doing anything against her will. Her engagement to Paul had been announced after an eighteen-
month courtship, during which time Tessa had weighed
and measured her feelings and considered them adequate.
If *adequate* was not quite the term a bride normally applied to her feelings for her groom, Tessa managed to
push that small issue to the back of her mind.

But that lack of certainty was what fogged her brain

now. How, at this late stage, could she be certain everything was going to be all right? But then again, why shouldn't it be? There had been so much thought and planning put into this wedding. She felt as if she'd been presented with a complicated geometry problem but had no understanding of basic theorems.

Her mother's frantic activity wasn't helping. Rosalind was behaving like a five-star general on the eve of a great campaign. Her battle plan consisted of a heavy schedule of last-minute tasks for everyone.

Not even Lydia was to escape. She had been delegated the task of tying the gold gauze bows around the starched damask serviettes. As well, she had to check the names inscribed in gold on the elegant place-cards against Rosalind's list of guests. Tessa thought that her grandmother was accepting these demands with surprising good grace.

Apparently Isaac had already left on one of Rosalind's missions. Rosalind, of course, had a host of tasks that only she could oversee. They mainly involved checking on everyone else. There was a final inspection with Gardeners and Greene, who were putting up the marquee and setting out all the tables and chairs. Once Rosalind was happy everything was going ahead according to her plans, Isaac would continue on the supervision there as her deputy. The caterers had to be consulted to ensure that there were no last-minute hitches with staff or at the markets where most of the ingredients would be purchased.

It was going to be a mammoth affair. On the afternoon of the reception, the chef, with an entourage of fourteen kitchen hands and servers and three truckloads of equipment, would be descending on Queen's Gardens.

Then there were the florists. Rosalind had orders with three different companies, and it was imperative that all

the flowers she'd ordered were available at her exact spec-
ified times.

'Mum, surely I should be doing more? You've taken
on so many tasks,' Tessa argued. 'I feel guilty swanning
around with nothing to do.'

'Nonsense,' insisted Rosalind. 'You should concentrate
on yourself and your groom and leave practical details to
me. And as you seem to be feeling so much better, perhaps you'd like to drive your own car to the beauty parlour today.'

The thought of a day to herself, free to move around
independently, cheered Tessa no end.

'Now you go off and enjoy all the beauty treatments
I've arranged,' Rosalind said, offering her daughter a
quick hug. 'You've been booked for a massage, a facial,
a manicure and a pedicure. We must have you absolutely
radiant from tip to toe on the most important day in your
life.'

And so Tessa emerged from her shower with a deter-
mination to make the best of a day of imposed self-
indulgence. As she dressed, she selected her favourites.
Over delicate, pale blue designer lingerie, she slipped a
powder blue cotton tweed jacket and slim matching skirt.
The deep V neck of the jacket was edged in dainty scal-
lops. Tessa loved the way this suit hugged her body in
just the right places, and she always felt especially feminine and glamorous when she wore it. And she knew it
accentuated the deep blue of her eyes.

Looking good was the first step to feeling good, she
told herself.

And by midafternoon she had to be looking even better.
She was in the hands of an amazing expert. After several
hours and a range of treatments, the beautician, Maggie,
finally stepped back and admired her handiwork, her

heavily lashed eyes round with delight. 'It is not often I get to achieve perfection.' She sighed dreamily. 'You're simply glowing. Oh, you gorgeous doll, you're going to be such an exquisite bride!'

Tessa smiled at her reflection in the mirror. The compliment was extravagant, but she couldn't help feeling pleased.

It was during the attentions of the manicurist that the telephone call came. Tessa's nails had been cut and filed and buffed, and her fingers were splayed to enable the second coat of lacquer to dry. Her feet were elevated, and each delicately lacquered toenail was separated from the next by fluffy balls of cotton wool.

'A call for Miss Morrow,' one of the young assistants announced.

'Oh, it's a bit difficult for me to move right now,' Tessa laughed. 'Who is it, Carrie? Is it important?'

'It's a man,' the woman replied, her eyes lit with interest. 'I think it might be your fiancé.'

'Oh, Paul? Then I guess I should think about answering it,' Tessa replied in an attempt at the kind of light banter that she'd been hearing around her in the salon all day.

'I'll wheel your chair over to the phone,' offered the manicurist, Heather. 'We really need a few cellular phones for these situations. I must speak to the manager about it.'

Tessa made her inelegant journey across the salon and accepted with a light-hearted giggle the receiver, which Carrie tucked between her shoulder and her cheek.

'Hello, Paul,' she said lightly.

'I'm afraid this isn't Paul, Tessa.'

The deep, resonant tones were definitely not Paul's. Tessa's heartbeats picked up pace.

'Isaac?' she stammered.

'Yes. I was wondering how much longer you're going to be? I need to talk to you.'

Tessa's head jerked in alarm, and the phone slipped from her shoulder. With difficulty, she replaced it. 'Talk?' she echoed, feeling foolish. What on earth could Isaac want to talk about?

There was a heavy silence at the other end of the line. 'There's something important I need to clear up with you before you—before tomorrow.'

Tessa closed her eyes as if somehow that would hold in the surge of emotion she felt. Surely she couldn't deal with anything else involving Isaac now. 'I don't think there's anything left for us to say, Isaac. We've tried to talk on two occasions already—at lunch the other day and then in the evening.' She glanced guiltily around the salon, but everyone was discreetly busy. 'We'll only end up fighting,' she whispered.

'Tessa, please. This is...' He paused, and Tessa was surprised by the desperate sigh that ended his silence. 'This is something I have to get off my chest. And we have so little time. Meet me as soon as you can,' Isaac insisted.

Don't do this, her common sense warned her. *You can't afford any more complications at this late stage.* But in the next breath, she couldn't help asking, 'Where?'

'I'll be on *Antares,* at the marina.' He cleared his throat. 'I know this sounds like a low-grade spy film or something, but it's the only place in this town where we can be fairly sure we won't be spotted by someone who knows our—your family.'

A dozen wild reasons for going to Isaac flashed through Tessa's mind. But she just as quickly cancelled each one out. It would be useless. He still showed her at every chance he could that he despised her. And anyhow, what did it matter? Whatever he had to say could make no difference now. Within twenty-four hours she would be married to Paul.

'I don't think it's a very good idea, Isaac.'

'Tessa, as I said, this is important.'

There was a considerable pause. 'I'm sorry. I can't come,' she said quietly before gingerly replacing the receiver in its cradle, taking care not to spoil her nails.

'Everything all right?' Heather asked as she inspected Tessa's nails.

'Fine.' Tessa nodded, blinking fiercely. 'I hope I haven't smudged anything after all the wonderful work you've done.'

'No.' The woman smiled. 'We're just about finished, anyhow.'

Tessa looked down at her elegant hands and feet. It was nice to be pampered.

She thought again of her beautiful wedding gown and how much she enjoyed the luxurious caress of its cool silk over her body and the swish of its skirt rustling to the floor. Getting married was a very glamorous occasion. It only happened once, and she knew that she was expected to make the most of it. She was glad she hadn't let Isaac destroy the new sense of serenity she'd been gradually building around her at the salon.

By the time she emerged from the change room, once more dressed in her chic blue suit with matching shoes, she felt cleansed, relaxed and attractive—better than she had for weeks. Carrie, the young assistant, hurried to her.

'Miss Morrow?'

'Yes?'

'Your fiancé is here to collect you.'

Tessa frowned. 'Paul's here? He mustn't know I have my car with me.'

'Well, he has perfect timing. You're all ready for him.' The manicurist grinned.

'Thanks to you,' Tessa followed the woman towards the salon's reception area.

As they entered the foyer through a latticed archway swathed in artificial roses, the manicurist pivoted on one foot and swung to Tessa. 'Mm, lucky you,' she murmured. 'I guessed your fiancé would be pretty dishy, but this stud takes the cake. Where'd you find him?'

Tessa followed the woman's gaze, then froze.

Isaac stood just inside the front door. He walked towards them, smiling confidently, but he halted abruptly in front of Tessa, staring at her, his dark eyes shimmering. 'Tess, you look—' He shook his head, apparently lost for words, his eyes fixed on her hungrily.

'She's stunning, isn't she? Just wait till you see her tomorrow,' Carrie laughed.

'Stunning—that's the word,' he said, recovering quickly. 'I'm stunned.'

Carrie heaved another deep, extravagant sigh. 'Oh, this is too, too romantic. I feel all gooey and emotional.'

Tessa winced. How could she let this embarrassing misconception continue? 'But, Carrie, this isn't my—' she began.

Before she could finish, Isaac stepped quickly to her and slipped his arm around her shoulders. 'I'm sorry to hurry you away, darling, but we still have so much to do.'

Carrie was beaming, and other members of the salon quickly gathered to wish Tessa well.

She had never been one for making scenes, but Tessa felt seriously inclined to create a spectacle. Surely it was a simple matter of ignoring the tantalising whiff of Isaac's aftershave, which teased her nostrils with its familiar, special allure. Surely she should pull away from his arm as it snugly enveloped her shoulders? Then she could announce to everyone that this man they were ogling was an imposter—not her fiancé at all.

She smiled stiffly at the circle of onlookers, knowing that she was a coward. When they saw her wedding photo in the newspaper, this gathering of women would be very curious. Tongues would certainly wag. But now was not the time to start a complicated series of explanations.

'Thanks so much, everyone,' she called as Isaac waved to their admiring, smiling faces and led her towards the salon doors. And Isaac and Tessa left with an enthusiastic chorus of good wishes ringing in their ears.

But as soon as they reached his car, parked a short distance down the street, Tessa wrenched away from him. 'Just what do you think you're playing at?' she cried. 'I told you I don't want to discuss anything with you. And how dare you pretend to be Paul.'

He raised his shoulders in the briefest of shrugs. 'And I told you it's important that I speak to you. You would have turned me away if I had admitted who I really was.'

Tessa nodded energetically. 'Of course I would.' She sighed. 'For heaven's sake, Isaac, what is it that's so pressing you have to discuss it right now?'

'We can't talk about it here. Please, Tessa. I need to explain something important.' He paused and looked briefly at the stream of traffic filing past them, before adding, 'It's to do with why I went away.'

Tessa blinked, and her hand flew instinctively to her chest. On any other day in the last wretched nine years, this was exactly what she wanted to hear, but not now. Now she wanted to stay calm and prepared for tomorrow. How dare Isaac! 'Surely it's far too late for that now,' she cried, stepping away from him.

Isaac ignored her protests. 'I can drive you, or you can

bring your car, but I don't want to discuss our private lives here in the middle of the street.' His hand reached out to her, and he frowned as she recoiled from him. 'Are you coming, Tessa?'

CHAPTER NINE

TESSA watched Isaac stride swiftly to the driver's side of his truck, giving the faithful Devil a scruff as he passed. Of course, there was no way she would sneak off to the boat with him on the eve of her wedding, like they had when they were foolish teenagers. Rosalind was expecting her home. No doubt Paul would be there, as well.

Isaac's hand reached the door handle. And suddenly from somewhere beyond all reason, Tessa heard herself say softly, 'All right, I'll come.'

He swerved to stare at her.

'But I'll drive to the marina in my own car.'

Isaac nodded, his face unreadable. Without speaking and without looking back, he swung into the driver's seat.

This is madness, she scolded herself as she drove towards The Strand. But sanity or commonsense had never guided her decisions regarding Isaac. He had only to beckon, and she would come running.

When Tessa reached the car park next to the marina, he was leaning against the side of his truck and scratching Devil's head, watching her steer her trim white sedan into a nearby parking spot. As she emerged from the car, his eyes lingered on her long legs before he glanced away again. Then, as she walked over to him, it seemed he needed to look at her again.

Her chest tightened.

'You look so elegant and so damn sensual in that outfit,' he said as she stood in front of him.

'Thank you,' she replied shakily.

125

He seemed to be taking in every detail of her appearance. And while the trip to the beauty parlour had been for Paul's benefit, there was a secret revengeful joy in seeing just how hungrily Isaac eyed the fullness of her freshly painted lips and the swell of her breasts revealed by the scooped neckline of her jacket. But she couldn't afford to allow his interest to fluster her. Now was certainly not the time for flirting. Instead, she stood in front of him, regarding him warily, her face tight with caution, while the cool wind skimming across the harbour flicked and played with her hair.

'Okay, Isaac. What is it you have to tell me? We'd better not take too long. It's already getting late.'

Isaac looked away. He stared at his wristwatch as if he had difficulty reading the dial. Then he indicated, with a nod, the steps leading to the pontoon where *Antares* was moored. He whistled softly to Devil, and the dog bounded over the side of the truck.

'Why is he coming?' she asked.

'He's a good watchdog,' Isaac muttered tersely as he headed for the pontoon.

She fell into step beside him.

As they reached her father's boat, she stopped and removed her high-heeled shoes. Standing before him, shoes in one hand, she repeated her question. 'So, what do you want to say?'

'Here, let me help you up first.'

She didn't try to prevent her skirt from riding high as she stepped onto the deck, then swung her long legs over the rail that edged the cockpit. However, she was enough of a sailor to land neatly, keeping her weight balanced so that she didn't have to fall against him.

'Stay here, Devil,' Isaac ordered his dog, and the faith-

ful animal obediently curled up in a shady corner of the
deck.

'Hasn't he ever disobeyed you?' she asked.

'No, never,' replied Isaac with an air of supreme confidence. 'Not since I trained him. But he was a fair little
mongrel as a pup.'

'Is that how he got his name?'

'Exactly.'

Isaac fitted the key to the cabin door, then offered a
hand to help Tessa down the companionway ladder. She
politely refused his hand, managing the simple descent
quite easily. Once in the cabin below, she stood stiffly,
watching him as he moved around, opening portholes and
letting in fresh air. Finally, Isaac slanted Tessa a searching
look.

'I was pretty close to the truth the other night, wasn't
I? You're not completely over the moon about this wedding tomorrow.'

The cheek of him! This was the last thing she needed
to hear! Tessa fumed. 'I hope you don't think I dragged
myself here just to chat about feelings that are none of
your business.'

His mouth twisted into a wry grimace as he tried again.
'Look, Tessa, I know my coming back has probably made
this week harder for you, but—'

Tessa felt bright spots of colour flare in her cheeks. By
contrast, she was surprised to hear the icy edge in her
voice as she replied. 'Please don't worry yourself about
me, Isaac. I got over you long ago.'

Wow! She hadn't expected to be able to say something
like that. But Isaac didn't look as chastened as he should.

The wind coming through a nearby porthole caught a
coil of her hair, whipping it across her eyes. Her finger
wound itself around the yellow strand. 'I've made a new

life for myself,' she said primly. 'I'm very content. My plans may not look particularly exciting to an outsider— an adventurer like you but this is how I want to live.' After a little break, she added, 'With Paul.'

He leant against a bench in the galley and folded his arms as he asked her quietly, 'If you're so deliriously happy with Paul, why all the agitation when I showed up on Monday?'

Full of indignation, she glared at him. 'What makes you think I cared? You're so full of yourself, Isaac Masters!'

But how could she pretend she didn't care? Rosalind had told everyone about the way she almost fainted when she'd heard Isaac was back, and then there'd been that disgraceful performance in his room the other night.

They stood still, facing each other like combatants in a boxing ring. Isaac's eyes travelled over her face. 'Do you really want me to remind you?' he asked.

Her chin lifted. 'I suppose you're talking about Wednesday night in, um, your bedroom,' she began bravely, but then she blushed and looked down. 'I guess I might still be a little attracted to you physically, but…'

'But?' Isaac echoed. Then he said very softly, 'But it's more than a little attraction, isn't it Tess? The other night, when I held you—'

He reached over as if he was going to tuck one of those stray strands of hair behind her ear. Just in time, he clenched his fist and shoved it into the pocket of his jeans.

Tessa bit her lip and stared through a porthole at the sunset-streaked sky. 'But all that physical business,' she said, shaking her head as she searched for the right words, 'that's not really what a good—a lasting marriage is about.'

'You believe that, Tess? You believe you can be happily married to one man while you feel physically very attracted to another?'

She lost her cool then. Clenching her fists, she shouted at him, 'You've got a nerve, Isaac! What have you dragged me here for? A sermon?'

'Not me. You've already heard all that from the priest. All those words, Theresa Rose, about to have and to hold, to love and to cherish.'

'For crying out loud, Isaac! You couldn't begin to understand something as serious as marriage. Concepts like commitment and fidelity don't exist in your vocabulary.' Tessa lifted her chin even more defiantly. 'Think about it. You pretended to love me. Then you ran away without so much as a goodbye. And after nine years you came back and started dating my best friend right under my very nose. And you have the hide to start lecturing me about *my* relationship!' Her voice broke on a furious sob.

Isaac's chuckle was tinged with a bitter note of self-mockery. 'I'm glad you mentioned Alice.'

'Alice?' That was unexpected. Tessa stared at Isaac, puzzled. Surely he wasn't going to be so brutal as to share with her the sordid details of his wonderful evening with her bridesmaid? 'What's Alice got to do with any of this?' she couldn't help asking.

'I had a very interesting conversation with her at dinner after the rehearsal last night. That's why I want to talk to you now.'

Tessa felt her cheeks grow cold. She looked around the cabin for somewhere to sit, and perched primly on the edge of a settee. Isaac joined her. If only he wouldn't sit so close!

'So what did you and Alice find so interesting to talk about?' she asked at last.

'You.'

A loud, incredulous laugh burst from Tessa's lips. 'Alice must have enjoyed that.'

Isaac shrugged and pulled a face.

'She was mega hot for *you*,' Tessa explained. 'The last thing she would have wanted to discuss was *me*.'

'She managed,' Isaac admitted with a sly grin. Then his face grew serious, and he stared at a wall decorated with framed photographs of the Morrow family enjoying happier times on the Great Barrier Reef. One picture showed Isaac and Tessa in their diving masks and snorkels. 'In fact,' he said softly, 'Alice told me the most important piece of news I've heard about you in the last nine years.'

Her eyes widened, and a jolt of something like hope slammed into her chest. 'What—what news was that, Isaac?'

He lifted his hand to hers. She hadn't realised she was fiddling with her hair again. As he spoke, he traced with his index finger the outline of her hand. 'Do you remember a conversation you had with Alice all those years ago? It was in the university library a few days before I ran— before I left town.'

Tessa frowned and tried to ignore the heady ripple of sensations aroused by his touch. Inappropriately, she wondered if he liked her newly glamorous nails.

'What were we talking about?'

'Me. You were discussing your feelings for me, to be precise.'

She snatched her hand away, alarmed. Of course she remembered the conversation. She remembered everything to do with Isaac with relentless clarity.

'Let me remind you.'

'No, it's okay. I remember.'

'Do you remember telling Alice that although you really liked me, you couldn't get serious about me? You couldn't possibly consider marrying me because nobody knew where I came from. I was a poor runaway, a street kid, a nobody.'

Tessa shook her head in angry disbelief. 'No, Isaac.'

'The correct answer is yes, Tessa,' he said with quiet emphasis.

'No. You've got it all wrong. Surely Alice didn't tell you that?'

'She didn't have to.'

'I don't understand.' Tessa gasped, struggling to breathe.

'I overheard that conversation, Tess. I was sitting at a study corral nearby.'

'You were eavesdropping?' She felt her head spinning. Her fingers clung to the wooden edge of the settee.

'I guess I was eavesdropping, but it was never intentional. My desk was hidden from the two of you by bookshelves. I hadn't even realised you were there until I heard you talking.'

Tessa sank against the bank of cushions behind her and drew in a long, slow, steadying breath. That conversation had always haunted her. She'd intensely regretted that those words ever left her lips.

But if she had known Isaac was listening!

'If you were there,' she cried, 'you would have heard what I said after that.'

Isaac shifted in his seat. 'I know that now, but you see, I didn't stay. Hell, Tess, the minute I heard you tell Alice you resented my background and could never really love me, I bolted. I was out of that library like a shot. I was too damned angry and upset to hang around.'

'Oh, Isaac. I'm so sorry.' Tessa tried to swallow the hard lump in her throat. She sniffed back tears. 'I had no idea. Did you really believe I meant what I said?'

'Blood oath, Tess. What do you think? I heard those statements with my own ears and from your lips. What was there to doubt?'

'You could have come and asked me about it, Isaac. I can't believe you never said anything to me—just took off. Oh, good heavens, Isaac! If only you had stayed you would have heard the rest of what I said, and then you might never have...' Tessa jumped up and swung to face Isaac, her hands flying to her face in horror. 'Oh, no! That's not why you left, is it? Tell me it wasn't because of what you overheard.'

He leant back and looked at her, shaking his head slowly.

'No, Tess. Well, not directly, anyhow. Can you imagine me simply stomping off and sulking like a kicked cat because I didn't like what I heard?'

'It's not a picture that leaps into my mind,' she admitted with a tiny smile.

'I'm sure I would have challenged you about it once I got a grip on myself,' he said.

Tessa sat again and leant towards him. 'But you didn't say a thing, Isaac, apart from all the anger you heaped on me the day you left.'

'I accused you of being a snob.'

'I think your vocabulary was more colourful than that.'

He grimaced. 'No doubt. But Tessa, you've no idea. All these years I've had this picture of you as a spoiled, stuck-up tease who'd played with my feelings for light entertainment.' His voice echoed regret, as though he still fielded a heavy slug of guilt for the pain he'd inflicted at their parting, and his expression softened, as if memories of their most precious moments were unravelling in his mind.

'And all these years, I never understood anything about

this,' Tessa whispered. She tried to blink into focus the blurry lights flickering to life in the marina beyond the porthole. But all she could see was Isaac's dark, rugged profile beside her. She couldn't help it. She had to reach out and touch him. Her hand shook as she gently laid a finger against his cheek. 'Oh, Isaac, how could you have doubted it? I was only trying to put Alice off the track, because I knew Mum used to quiz her about us all the time.'

He sat very still as her finger traced the shadowy outline of his jaw while she spoke. 'If only you'd waited a few minutes more—you would have heard me take everything back. Heavens above! I told Alice that I didn't mean any of it. I explained how I knew Mum was unhappy about my being with you all the time, but I didn't care. She could never come between us. I told her I loved you....'

Isaac's hand clasped her finger against his mouth, and he kissed the perfectly manicured berry-coloured nail. 'I know all that *now*,' he said. 'According to our good friend Alice, you claimed that we were soul mates.'

'That's exactly what I said,' Tessa cried, slowly uncurling the other fingers of her hand and watching him kiss each one tenderly. 'I told her you were a part of me.'

Isaac smiled a slow, sad smile, and when he had finished kissing her fingers, he closed his hand over hers, holding it tightly. 'You said we were a single entity.'

'Did Alice tell you that, too?' Her voice was scratchy.

'Yes, she claims she's always remembered everything you said that day, because she thought it was so amazingly romantic.' Isaac smiled, but as he held her hand on his knee, there was no mockery in his expression.

'Good heavens,' commented Tessa, surprised. 'I thought Alice had a rather jaundiced view of romance.

When soppy movies make most of us reach for a tissue, she usually says she wants to grab for a bucket to be sick.'

His shoulders rose in a shrug. 'Well, it seems your admission made a lasting impression. Alice swears it was so moving there were white doves fluttering round the library, roses blossoming on the bookshelves, violins playing…the whole rhapsody.'

Something approaching a giggle escaped from Tessa. 'I did get a bit melodramatic. I so much wanted to take back what I'd said. It felt so bad pretending I didn't love you.'

'It felt very bad hearing it, too.'

Tessa stared at Isaac. In the cabin it was so quiet and still she could hear her heart pounding. 'I'm sorry,' she whispered.

How could a man look so sad and yet so sexy? She wanted to hang on to the moment, a moment of peace, of reconciliation, possibly a turning point. But there was another question she had to ask. 'Isaac, if it wasn't overhearing that conversation that made you leave, what on earth happened?' Fearfully, she watched him frown and shake his head. She grabbed his shoulder and shook it. 'You've got to tell me. Why did you go away? You said yesterday morning that it was for *my* sake. I deserve to know, Isaac.'

He pulled away from her grasp and leant forward abruptly, letting out air with a loud hiss through his teeth. 'Why?' He turned to her. 'Surely the answer is obvious?'

'If it is, I've been overlooking the glaringly obvious for the past nine years.'

She waited for him to say something.

'No.' He shook his head decisively. 'I've told you as much as I intended to, Tessa.' He stood up and walked away from her to stare through another porthole at the inky, star-spangled sky. He spoke with his back to her. 'I just needed to let you know that if my attitude has been a little distanced or critical this week, I'm sorry. I know now it wasn't warranted. But I've spent the last nine years believing you to be a cruel, heartless little bitch.' He grimaced as he turned to face her. 'I'm afraid my entire perspective was coloured by my misunderstanding.'

'But you're not going to answer my question?'

He tugged at the open collar of his shirt as if he needed more breathing space.

'No.' Isaac kicked at the leg of the chart table. 'It's too late, Tess. I don't think anything would be achieved by going over all that history at this point in time. I'm sorry,' he said again gruffly, 'but it's too complicated and too late.'

She moved to stand beside him. In the confines of the cabin, tantalising drifts of his clean, freshly showered and shaved skin enveloped her.

'So,' she said, 'all you wanted to tell me was that you used to think I didn't love you, but now you realise I do.'

'Pardon?' His Adam's apple jerked in his throat.

'I—I mean I *did* love you,' she stammered. 'You know now that I used to love you—when I was nineteen. That's what you wanted to say, is it?'

'I thought I'd managed more than that.' He looked at her and frowned as his eyes fixed on the trembling of her bottom lip and her chin. 'Surely that isn't all it boils down to?' he asked.

'I don't know, Isaac. You drew up the agenda for this meeting.' She looked straight into his eyes, which were as inky as the night-black sea and sky. But his expression was so desperately sad, she felt an overwhelming urge to comfort him.

'Somehow I wanted this conversation to help you,' he sighed.

'Help me?'

'Yes. I guess I didn't want to let you get married to-morrow without apologising for my attitude—without letting you know I'd jumped to all sorts of wrong conclusions. I didn't want you weighed down by any emotional baggage of my making.'

Tessa slumped onto the settee. *Was* that the truth? What else could she expect? That he would want to steal her away from her fiancé? Of course not! She should have been delighted, relieved, grateful.

'Oh, Isaac. I'm not sure that this has helped at all.'

'Then I must be doubly apologetic.'

She looked away, offering him a view of her delicate profile. Then she took a deep breath and faced him again. 'I can't help wondering if you're telling me in a round-about way that you still—that your feelings for me haven't died, after all.'

Oh, sweet heaven! He was staring at her with the same stunned expression he might have worn if she'd suddenly turned green and sprouted antennae. He rapidly switched his gaze out to sea and appeared to watch with great attention the blinking starboard lights that indicated the passage of a yacht up the channel.

'Don't waste your time wondering about my feelings,' he said crisply.

'I see.' Somehow she managed to produce a cold, distant ring of acceptance in her tone.

He sighed. 'We can't afford this kind of conversation, Tessa.'

To her dismay, Tessa could not stop the tears that welled in her eyes. As she shook her head at Isaac, twin rivulets rolled down her cheeks. 'You mean we should hide from the truth?'

He handed her a folded white handkerchief.

She took it and scrubbed at her cheeks, then twisted the square of Irish linen in her fingers, studying the embroidered *I* in the corner.

'The truth?' he asked bitterly, then paused. 'The truth,' he continued, 'is that tomorrow you will become Mrs. Paul Hammond. I would never consider asking you to change that situation.' And, as if to underline his certainty, he folded his arms. 'I learnt many years ago that Queen Tess is out of my league.'

And then she knew he was hiding from the truth. 'Don't try to hand me that line now, Isaac,' she cried. 'We've already laid that particular ghost.'

He wanted her! Tessa knew it, and she wasn't about to let him go again without showing him beyond doubt how she felt. She drifted across the short gap between them, slowly, seductively, like a siren floating out of a misty sea. Stopping too close to him, she held his gaze. 'You know that you only have to kiss me to prove that's not true,' she said.

His breathing was ragged.

So was hers.

He began to smile and shake his head, as if he wanted to deny everything she said, but then, as if hypnotised, he paused.

Tessa's heart sang. She knew Isaac needed to make love to her as much as she needed him. His hand slowly came up to tilt her chin, and his mouth stooped towards her. As his lips reached hers, his hands pulled her against him, and he moaned softly.

Knowing this might be her only chance to kiss Isaac again, Tessa threw her arms around his neck, drawing his mouth deep into hers. Never had he tasted so devastatingly sexy. How easily his lips and tongue stirred her senses, till every nerve ending trembled with need. And when his body strained against her, hard and heavy, she felt her own response mounting rapidly low inside her.

Isaac invaded her mouth as if he owned it, and she surrendered to his possession with an impatience born of long suffering. Their world contracted to the small yacht's cabin, to the circle of Isaac's arms, and nothing, absolutely nothing else in the universe mattered.

In mere seconds, his hand found the soft mound of her breast and his fingers released the buttons of her designer jacket to reveal, in the moonlight, the matching powder blue lace beneath.

'Let's move,' he muttered, steering her through the galley into the aft cabin. She clung to him, afraid to be separated even for a moment, fearful that he might pull away and accuse her of faithlessness again. And she continued to scatter a shower of kisses over his neck and to nibble at his ear, distracting them both completely from any last chance at commonsense.

They reached the wide bunk, and he sat down and pulled her savagely onto him.

Tessa sank against him, and her body fitted perfectly with his as if it had found its home. The night air from an open hatch above was cool on her breasts and shoulders as she shrugged off the jacket.

'Please,' she whispered. The blue lace underwear was released from its clasp, and at last she felt Isaac's hot mouth on her bare breasts. She shuddered with pleasure, arching towards him in a gesture of unrestrained offering.

'Oh, Isaac,' she cried softly.

He groaned, kissed her again and cupped her breasts more possessively, his circling thumbs driving her impatiently to a feverish peak of longing. She felt her body surge with a starved hunger, tired of waiting.

She fleetingly marvelled that everything happened so

effortlessly. There was nothing awkward or jarring to hinder them or to give them time for second thoughts. Her skirt rode over her hips just as easily as the blue lace panties slid down, and shortly afterwards, she heard the scrape of the zip of Isaac's jeans. And suddenly they were together again, his urgent, thrusting masculinity filling her. Silken and welcoming, her body grasped him tightly, sharing his pleasure and his urgency. His lips trailed up her neck, slid along her jaw and finally met her lips, sealing them as surely as his body sealed with hers.

There wasn't time for guilt before she was consumed by a delicious sensory overload. This was Isaac, her Isaac. Oh! How she had missed his loving! There was nothing in the world that compared to this perfect intimacy. She buried her face in the warmth of his neck as a swirling tide lifted her and swept her along on a wave of exquisite sensation. His lips found hers again as the sensation claimed her, consumed her soul and catapulted her forwards triumphantly, insistently, till at last it released her, gasping and breathless.

She clung to Isaac, quivering with dazzling joy, and listened as his laboured breathing slowly steadied again.

Resting her damp head against his shoulder, Tessa heard the thudding of his heart echo her own.

'Oh, Isaac,' she sighed. 'That was... It was...' She paused, searching for the right words to convey the absolute height and depth of her feelings at that moment.

'That was some parting gift,' he said heavily, easing away from her.

Tessa's heartbeat stilled, then galloped chaotically. 'Parting?' she whispered, unable to prevent her voice from trembling. 'This is goodbye?'

'What else can it be?' he said grimly as he wrenched his clothes into order.

She tried to swallow. Her throat felt constricted by sudden hot tears. 'Couldn't it be a reunion?' she asked, glad of the darkness in the unlit cabin as she struggled to arrange her skirt and jacket. 'After all this time, it felt more like a greeting to me.'

She heard his empty chuckle. 'What's so funny?' she almost screamed, reaching for him. But he stood abruptly. Her hand slid down his leg and landed on the edge of the bunk.

'Let's call it hello and goodbye,' he said as he turned and stepped quickly through the cabin away from her. 'Goodbye, Isaac, hello, Paul.'

Horrified, she stumbled after him. 'You still want me to marry Paul?' she asked. 'You planned to make love to me and then hand me over to someone else just as easily?'

'You're wrong on both counts,' he growled. 'In the first place, I never planned to make love to you. What happened just now was the unfortunate, spontaneous coupling of two unthinking fools. Secondly, Tessa, it is you who chose to marry Paul Hammond. I have no say in the matter whatsoever. I certainly didn't come here tonight with the intention of changing your mind.'

'Oh,' Tessa moaned pitifully, 'I don't know what you intended, Isaac, but I couldn't—oh, dear God, what am I going to do?'

He stood in silence on the darkened step, staring at her. *Please help me,* she entreated silently. *Please, Isaac. Tell me you want me. Don't leave me again.* 'What should I do?' she whispered.

'You are going to go home to your family,' he said. 'Rosalind will most probably have engaged the State Emergency Services to launch a full-scale search for you by now.'

The thought of Rosalind stilled her as effectively as if

she'd run headlong into an invisible force-field. How would she explain being so late to her mother?

How would she explain any of this? She couldn't understand it herself. As she stood there, trembling with the aftermath of their passion, an explanation of how something so extraordinary had happened or what it meant escaped her entirely.

'How can you be so heartless?' she asked.

'My heart has collected so much scar tissue that it doesn't notice the odd knock any more,' he growled as he backed away from her.

'But, Isaac—what we just shared?' she asked, her voice faint and bewildered.

'Was an act of foolishness best forgotten quickly,' replied Isaac.

'You can do that?' she cried, all sense of pride abandoned long ago. 'You can make love to me and then walk away and forget about it as if it never happened?'

He stood at the bottom of the companionway stairs and stared at her for long, slow seconds. His dark hair was tousled, emphasising the lean, rugged lines of his face. Through the companionway hatch, a square of jet black night sky framed him, making him look savage, wild and untamed. From another world.

Tell me you can't leave me again, she pleaded silently.

'As things stand, I have no alternative,' he said flatly, as if all his energy had departed. He took one step towards her, then stopped. 'What do you want me to do, for God's sake? You've made it very clear to me on several occasions that you definitely want to marry the tuba-playing attorney and for the best of reasons. You've made your bed, Tessa. But—but I won't be lying in it.'

She stared at him hopelessly, finally accepting the dreadful logic of his words. He was right. She had ac-

cepted Paul's proposal. No one had forced her into this
marriage, and it was far too late to back out now. The
mere thought of telling Rosalind that the whole affair was
cancelled was unthinkable. If Isaac had given her any indication that he loved her or wanted to be her life partner,
perhaps she could find the courage to face Rosalind. And
Paul.

But now, on the eve of her wedding, with Isaac's rejection of their lovemaking as a foolish mistake ringing
in her ears, it all seemed rather pointless.

In silence they closed up the boat, and with leaden feet,
she followed him along the pontoon to the car park. They
didn't speak until they reached their vehicles.

'You drive home alone,' Isaac suggested. 'Everyone
will be frantic enough without arousing further suspicion
by our arriving together.'

Tessa nodded numbly and set her key in the ignition.
Her mind seethed with fragments of disjointed thoughts.
Isaac had said nothing about loving her. Her car's engine
sprang to life, and she backed it out of the parking bay.
He never once indicated that he wanted her for himself.

She drove through the city and headed up the hill to
home. And she had to think of Paul. Surely he didn't
deserve to be jilted?

It was Paul who was waiting on the footpath when she
pulled into the kerb. Tessa was shocked by the way her
heart sank when she saw him standing there, just outside
the pool of yellow light cast by the street lamp. Surely
dismay shouldn't be the reaction of a bride for her groom
on the eve of their wedding? She was already feeling
guilty, but now her stomach churned even more uncomfortably.

As she stepped out of her car, Paul hurried forward.

Frowning, he looked at her sharply, and snapped, 'You're very late.'

'They botched up my manicure,' she replied just a little too quickly. 'Had to start all over again. You've no idea how long it takes—all those coats.'

In the lamplight, she could see the sceptical lift of his eyebrow. Tessa had a dreadful suspicion that Rosalind had called the salon and that Paul knew she was lying, but to her relief, he didn't challenge her. He simply put an arm around her shoulders and commented, 'I am always astounded by the effort and pain you women put yourselves through—'

A sudden beeping interrupted him, and he turned away and whipped a mobile phone out of his breast pocket.

'Yes?' he barked.

Tessa hovered uncertainly on the footpath.

'What do you mean it's leaked out?' he snapped into the phone.

'Would you like me to go inside?' she whispered, but Paul was far too distracted by the voice on the other end of the line.

'If this bloody thing's comes unstuck, we're all finished.' He turned his back to her, listening intently to the phone. Then he glanced at her over his shoulder, and his voice dropped. 'Hell, no. I for one don't want to be disbarred,' he growled.

'I'll go and see Mum,' Tessa told his hunched back, and began to hurry up the front path. Although she was stunned by Paul's violent exchange with the mystery caller, she was grateful to be able to slip inside, to escape without explanation of her evening's activities.

Paul had lowered his voice, but as she hurried away, his words were very clear in the still night air. 'I don't need reminding that it was my idea,' he said. 'But you were happy to come along for a quick profit.'

She was puzzling over the disturbing conversation when she found her mother in the kitchen. If Paul's reception had been any different from what Tessa expected, Rosalind's was entirely predictable. She was fit to burst.

'Tessa!' Her voice was shrill. 'We've been going out of our minds with worry.'

'I'm sorry, Mum,' Tessa replied wearily. 'I just drove down to The Strand for a little while. I needed some time out—some time just to think for a bit.'

'Think?' Rosalind's dark eyes narrowed. 'On the eve of your wedding?'

'It's all been so hectic,' Tessa said defensively.

Paul walked into the kitchen, and she shot him a beseeching look, hoping for his support. This kind of attack from her mother, as if she were still a young teenager who'd broken her curfew, was more than she could handle right now.

But Paul was looking at her with a very startled expression, and his round grey eyes bulged as they roved over her blue suit, making her uncomfortably aware of the low neckline and the tight skirt. 'You were down on The Strand dressed like *that?*' he asked. 'I thought you had more sense of decency.'

'For heaven's sake, Paul, I've worn this suit out with you before today. You never objected then. What do you think I was doing? Streetwalking?'

Paul's upper lip curled. 'I can't say I'm wrapped in the idea of my bride parading all alone along the beach front looking like a—'

'I wasn't *parading* anywhere.' Tessa flung the words at him. But she felt her cheeks burn as she thought of exactly what she had been doing. She was aware of her mother's suspiciously curious eyes. Tessa realised with alarm that the look in those eyes held more than suspicion. Her mother's expression was wary, even frightened.

'Now, now, *children*,' Rosalind interjected nervously. 'Let's not start bickering. I think you're both getting unnecessarily tense. How about I put the kettle on? And Tessa, I have a bowl of pasta left over from dinner that I'll heat in the microwave for you.'

'Thanks, Mum.' Tessa sank onto a kitchen stool and rested her elbows on the bench top. Paul took a deep breath and came and sat beside her.

'You're right, as always, Rosalind,' he said wearily. 'I *am* unnecessarily tense. All these dreadful business problems have blown up at exactly the wrong time.'

Tessa forced herself to sound concerned. 'Is this all connected with that court case yesterday? The one that held you up?'

Paul looked startled. 'What do you know about that?' His voice was thin and sharp.

'Absolutely nothing,' said Tessa. 'I was simply trying to show some interest in your problems.'

Paul slumped beside her and patted her hand. 'Of course, my dear. I'm sorry.' Rosalind handed them each a mug of tea and placed a bowl of chicken and mushroom fettucini in front of Tessa. And then she left them alone in the kitchen.

As she sipped her tea and stirred the pasta with her fork, Tessa willed herself to forget about Isaac. She had to. They had absolutely no future. And she hoped fervently that she would bring Paul pleasure in his bed the following night. He didn't deserve a loveless marriage.

CHAPTER TEN

WEDDING day...

Tessa sat in her parents' bedroom and examined the image in the oval glass before her. After a morning at the hairdresser's, her fair hair was drawn back in a series of fine braids and caught in a low knot. Tiny spirals had been loosened around her face to soften the overall effect. She was surprised that after a week of restless nights spent tossing and turning, she looked unexpectedly good—dreamily romantic perhaps, but not quite radiant.

'You look very elegant, very bridal,' said Alice as she admired Tessa's reflection in the mirror.

Smiling at Alice, whose dark curls had been gathered into a similarly old-fashioned knot, she replied, 'And you look lovely—very demure, just as my bridesmaid should.'

'I feel like I'm ready for a part in a movie—a historical romance,' Alice laughed.

Dressed in their petticoats—bridal white for Tessa, coffee silk for Alice—and with their make-up complete, they were preparing to don their dresses for the photographs before the ceremony.

'I love my bridesmaid's dress,' Alice said, looking at the slim-line coffee lace number that hung on a nearby wardrobe door. 'But this is a gown to die for.' She crossed to Tessa's beautiful wedding dress on its hand-embroidered hanger. 'I just love this heavenly train, the way it floats behind you...and these darling little pale pink rosebuds. This dress just has to epitomise every bride's dream.'

'Alice, calm down,' Tessa laughed, deliberately ignoring the less than calm knots in her stomach. 'You sound like you're still in front of the television cameras.'

'Do I?' asked Alice, appalled. 'It's a bad habit. I do it when I'm nervous.'

'Nervous?' asked a surprised Tessa. 'What on earth do you have to be nervous about? I'm the one getting married.'

'Precisely,' replied Alice, looking at her friend rather enigmatically from beneath her mascara-thickened lashes.

'So?' persisted Tessa, her stomach tightening another impossible notch.

'Oh, Lord, Tessa. I don't even know how to begin to say this. I've been trying to blurt it out all morning. I *am* nervous about you....'

Alice's sunny features suddenly clouded. Her merry brown eyes grew dark and sombre, and her perky mouth developed a distinct droop.

The sight was enough to make Tessa sit down abruptly on the edge of her parents' bed, her fingers restlessly roaming the quilted spread. All morning she'd held herself together with remarkable decorum, and she'd just about decided she was going to be able to pull this whole thing off.

'Perhaps you'd better not say anything,' she said to Alice, trying to keep her voice calm.

Alice looked at her feet, encased in their delicate stockings, and seemed engrossed by her toes as they toyed with the deep snowy pile of the bedroom carpet. Then her shrewd glance swept to Tessa. She stared solemnly at her friend and bit her lip.

'Dare I mention the name Isaac?' she asked.

Tessa's uncomfortable stomach lurched sickeningly,

and she felt her limbs tremble. 'I'd rather you didn't,' she managed to say after some time.

Alice dashed across the floor and plonked down on the bed beside her friend. 'Tessa, while you are still Tessa Morrow and before it's too damn late, you've got to be honest with yourself. I know the timing's horrendous, but for heaven's sake, darling, have you really thought about this? Have you thought that you might be making a terrible mistake?'

'Mistake?' echoed Tessa, her chest so tight she could hardly breathe.

'Yes! Mistake, error of judgement, blunder, oversight…call it what you like…fiasco of the century!'

'Please, Alice,' said Tessa. 'Don't be so melodramatic.'

'Oh, I'm sorry, darling,' cried Alice, flinging her arms around Tessa. 'You're shaking.' She hugged Tessa tight. 'I know this is very intrusive of me, honey, but I just have to ask you. Are you absolutely certain you want to marry Paul?'

Tessa tried to swallow the lump in her throat. If only she could jump up and cry triumphantly at Alice, *Yes! Yes! Yes! Of course I want to marry Paul! I love him!*

'That's a pretty stupid question to be asking me now,' she whispered.

'I know, sweetheart,' murmured Alice, taking Tessa's hands in hers and squeezing them gently. 'Honestly, I wouldn't buy into this line of questioning normally, but crikey, I'm your best friend. I've known you since the third grade. We've never had any secrets, and suddenly I've got this horrible feeling you're about to make your whole life one terrible big one.'

Tessa stared at Alice, blue eyes wide with fear fixed on brown ones round with anxiety.

'You should be marrying Isaac today, not Paul,' insisted Alice.

'N-no. I can't. You don't understand.'

'What don't I understand?' asked Alice gently. 'You'll have to convince me, Tess.'

Tessa closed her eyes as much to hold back the welling tears as to clarify her thinking. She thought she'd experienced every form of mental torment over the past week, but her emotions were more twisted and torn than ever. She was terrified that if she started to speak about this problem, the truth—the truth she hadn't the courage to face—might come rushing to the surface as inevitably as champagne bubbles erupted at the popping of a cork.

And yet, she realised with a sudden wash of loneliness, she needed to talk about this to Alice. It had been dreadful trying to deal with it alone.

'It's true,' she began hesitantly, 'that I still have strong feelings for Isaac. But they're only physical, and in any case, he doesn't want to marry me.'

Alice let out a low, unfeminine whistle followed by a very unladylike swearword. 'Tessa,' she said, sighing, 'will you listen to an investigative journalist give an almost unbiased report on this situation?'

'I—I guess so.'

'The truth of the matter—what everybody is overlooking, especially the parties most concerned—is that you and Isaac belong together like—like Bogart and Bergman in *Casablanca*, or Cathy and Heathcliff in *Wuthering Heights*. You've always loved each other. Neither of you has ever stopped loving the other. I soon discovered I didn't have a snowflake's hope in Hades with Isaac the other night. And believe me, I would have grabbed him for myself if I thought I'd had even half a chance.'

'But Alice, how can you possibly imagine Isaac loves

me when he left me without any explanation nine years
ago and he's never once contacted me? He told me him
self, the only reason he came back at all was to clear out
any emotional baggage so we can both get on with our
own lives.'

'I don't believe that for one moment,' replied Alice,
'but even if it were true, do you really think you should
tie yourself to Paul as an alternative?'

'That's the difficult bit.' Tessa sighed. It was only half
the truth. Pretending she didn't love Isaac with every
ounce of her being was as difficult as breathing without
air, but pretending she loved Paul was an issue she could
no longer avoid. 'I don't want to hurt Paul,' she moaned.

'You don't want to hurt Paul today,' said Alice. 'But
what about next week, next year, in twenty years' time?
If you don't love him and he has to live with you, real-
ising that you're pretending, won't you hurt him much,
much more?'

'Perhaps,' whispered Tessa and immediately burst into
a terrible flood of tears. Tears that acknowledged the ap-
palling truth of Alice's words. Not gentle tears that
wouldn't smudge her make-up, but rasping, hideously
noisy sobs that came welling up from the pain deep inside
her, bursting out of her mouth, forcing her shoulders to
heave violently.

'Poor baby,' whispered Alice, stroking her jerking
shoulders, sounding even to Tessa's distraught ears rather
frightened of the despair she'd unleashed.

Dimly, over the sound of her sobbing, Tessa heard her
father's voice coming from the doorway.

'Just popping up to see how you two—' He stopped.

She knew he was waiting for some kind of explanation,
but there was no way she could respond.

'Tessa, dear?' She heard him falter as he crossed the room hurriedly.

Then somehow, as his hand touched her cheek, she managed to reply, her voice sounding agonised and ugly. 'Oh, Dad,' she sobbed, 'please help me. I—I don't know what to do.'

His weight made the bed sink a little as he sat beside her and drew her to him gently. And as her father's arms cradled her and she felt the familiar warmth of his chest against her cheek, the racking sobs continued to tear their way out of Tessa's throat. Above her head, she heard him speak to Alice. 'This is all about Isaac, isn't it?' he asked quietly.

Alice didn't need to answer. Tessa nodded against his chest and felt her father's long, deep sigh.

'You still love him, don't you, my dear?'

Tessa dragged her head up. She could just make out her father's gentle face through the blur of tears. 'Yes,' she said, her voice trembling like the grass in the wind. But then with a surge of confidence, she added, 'Oh, yes, Dad, I've never stopped loving him.'

It felt so, so good to hear those words out in the open at long last.

'I've suspected this all along, of course. But your mother…' John Morrow compressed his lips tightly, as if considering the wisdom of speaking further.

'I know Mum's never been happy about us,' said Tessa.

Her father didn't reply, but sat with one arm around her, thoughtfully stroking her shoulder while he stared at the carpet and frowned, as if remembering Rosalind's litany of reasons for rejecting Isaac.

Tessa reached up to clasp her father's hand at her shoulder. She shook it gently. 'Dad, I can't…I'm sorry, but I can't marry Paul.'

Dr. Morrow nodded slowly.

Two things she'd said out loud. *I love Isaac. I can't marry Paul.* Tessa felt stronger. She stood up. 'I have to tell Mum.'

'Gulp!' exclaimed Alice. 'Do you want company?'

'I—I think I'll be all right.' Then she had second thoughts. 'Perhaps you'd better come, Dad. Mum's going to need you.'

She pulled her father from the bed and in her stockinged feet and petticoat ran out of the room and down the hall, searching for Rosalind. She found her in the kitchen, fixing Isaac's bow tie.

'Tessa! Good heavens, you're not dressed! You look terrible. What's happened?'

Tessa recoiled as she heard her mother's high-pitched voice. And at the sight of Isaac's face, frozen in a mask of utter stupor, her quivering lips could no longer form the words of her message. Then Dr. Morrow arrived, puffing, behind Tessa, and she clutched her father's hand tightly.

'Rosalind, my dear, I'm afraid—' Dr. Morrow began, then looked nervously at Isaac. 'Perhaps Isaac wouldn't mind...' he said, gesturing towards the door.

'Yeah, sure thing. I'm on my way,' replied Isaac shakily. 'I'll look after Lydia and I'll see you in church.' He shot another startled glance at each of them in turn, and his frowning gaze rested a little longer on Tessa, taking in her petticoat and her red and blotched face smeared with mascara. 'Be seeing you,' he said softly, and then turned abruptly to leave.

With the greatest of willpower, Tessa refrained from chasing after Isaac. Another little sob broke from her lips as his tall, dark frame disappeared through the doorway.

Dr. Morrow spoke. 'Rosalind, dear, I'm afraid we have a little problem.'

'Problem?' screeched Rosalind. Her hands flew shakily to her white face, and her eyes widened wildly. She shook her head in disbelief. 'Of course there's no problem. Everything is organised perfectly. This wedding will go off like clockwork.' As she spoke, she stared at Tessa's tear-streaked face. 'What have you done to yourself?' she cried. Then she whirled on her husband. 'How can we have a problem?'

Tessa took a deep breath. 'It's my fault, Mum. I—I'm terribly sorry, but I can't go ahead with the wedding.'

A strangled gasp broke from Rosalind.

Tessa's father cleared his throat. 'Rosalind, certain issues have come to a head. I know it's unfortunate to have to deal with it right now, but there are things we should have told Tessa long ago.'

'For pity's sake,' gasped Rosalind, pushing her husband away. 'Are you out of your mind? We haven't got time for raking up the past now. The photographer will be here any minute, and Tessa must be ready.'

She stepped towards Tessa and then halted abruptly, her shocked gaze taking in finally the full implications of her daughter's words and her ravaged appearance, her shaking shoulders and her red, blotchy, tear-swollen face.

Rosalind's red mouth opened and stayed open. She raised helpless hands to her face, and a sob broke from her lips. 'You're serious, aren't you?' she said at last.

John Morrow stepped forwards and placed a comforting arm around his wife's shoulders, his face full of compassion for her distress.

'Yes, I mean it, Mum,' Tessa said so softly she could scarcely hear her own voice. 'I can't marry Paul.'

'Oh,' said Rosalind just as quietly. She staggered against a kitchen bench. 'You're absolutely sure?'

'Yes, Mum. I'm sure. I'm sorry I've left it so late to tell you. Perhaps if Isaac hadn't come back…'

Rosalind shook her head again, as if to dismiss Tessa's apology.

'Come into the lounge, my dear. You need to sit down,' her husband suggested.

'No,' responded Rosalind suddenly. 'No, I'm all right. I'm *all right!*' She reached out shaking arms to Tessa, who sank into her mother's embrace. 'Oh, my poor darling,' she cried. 'What have I done to you?'

'You, Mum? You haven't done anything,' sobbed Tessa. 'It's me. I should never have agreed to marry Paul in the first place. I knew that I still loved Isaac. And— and just because he doesn't love me—that doesn't mean I should simply find someone else.'

'No, Tessa,' soothed Rosalind. 'Oh, my goodness. This *is* my fault.'

Tessa drew away from her mother, her mind full of desperate questions.

Rosalind raked long fingers through her expensively styled hair. She took a deep, shuddering breath and stared at the ceiling as she spoke. 'There's something I should have told you. Something I did a long time ago.' She paused. 'I would like to take my time explaining this.' She gestured helplessly. 'But I don't have time. We have to be practical. There's so much to do—caterers, photographers. Oh, dear Lord, they'll have a fit if we try to call this off now.'

A cough behind them distracted Rosalind. Alice stepped tentatively into the kitchen. 'Maybe I can help out with the cancellations?' she asked.

'Well, perhaps, dear,' agreed John Morrow, helping his wife onto a kitchen stool.

'I'd love to help,' responded Alice. 'Just give me a list of phone numbers, and I'll look after the caterers and anything else that needs to be done. I can be very charming when I want to and I can achieve miracles from one end of a phone line.'

'John, my diary is on my desk. Could you show Alice? Thank you, dear.'

'Of course.'

Alice and her father left the room, and Tessa looked expectantly at her mother. Despite the sick tension in her stomach, she was desperate to hear whatever she had to say.

And it seemed Rosalind was just as eager to off-load her confession. 'Darling,' she began. 'I'm so ashamed to admit this now, but I *forced* Isaac to leave us nine years ago.'

Tessa clutched the kitchen table for support.

'You see, I hated the thought of him falling in love with you, my precious baby—a boy from the gutter, with no prospects and a drug addict for a mother!'

'What did you do?' whispered Tessa.

Her face distorted with emotion, Rosalind went on. 'I told him he had to go right away from us without making a fuss. I actually lied and said your father had developed a heart condition. I told Isaac that if he tried to take you with him, or even upset you over this, it would probably kill your father. I—it was wicked of me, but I gambled on the enormous respect I knew he had for John. Tessa, I really am terribly ashamed of myself.'

Tessa stared. 'So that was why Isaac never explained why he left.'

Rosalind nodded and closed her eyes to hold back tears.

'Yes, sweetheart. He couldn't have told you his reason for leaving without revealing what a heartless and calculating snob your mother was.'

'He thought I was a snob, too,' murmured Tessa.

'I was wrong about Isaac, of course. I know that now. He really is quite a fine style of man,' Rosalind said softly. 'I won't ask you to forgive me, dear, but one day I hope you will.'

Tessa would have liked to reassure her mother immediately, but she felt too shocked and shaken to find the words. All she could think of was the pain Isaac must have suffered when he was sent away, thinking he was unworthy and convinced he had no hope of ever earning a right to her love.

The thought was unbearable.

At that moment, Alice burst into the room. 'Oh, Tess, Mrs. Morrow,' she gasped. Her face was flushed, and her eyes gleamed wildly.

'Alice, what is it? Have the caterers been difficult?' cried Rosalind.

'No, not at all. They've been quite remarkable,' Alice reassured her. 'No, this is something else entirely.' She paused and crossed the room to place a comforting arm around Tessa. 'I knew you'd made the right decision, Tess,' she said gently. 'But now I've had that confirmed in a most unexpected way. I just had a call from one of the fellows at work, and the story's just broken. Paul has been working as a lawyer with those shady businessmen who've been trying to buy half of South Townsville.'

'Good heavens!' gasped Rosalind.

'But there's worse,' continued a wide-eyed Alice. 'It's just been released that he was also *in league* with them!'

'Paul was involved in buying out the preschool's land?' Tessa cried.

Alice nodded. 'Probably he couldn't have gone ahead
with the wedding today even if you'd wanted him to. It
seems he has a lot more explaining to do in court. It's all
over some trust funds they were planning to use illegally.'

Stunned, Tessa and Rosalind stared at her in horrified
silence.

'This is unbelievable,' said Rosalind at last. Tessa
couldn't speak. She felt ill, as if she'd woken up in the
middle of some bizarre nightmare.

Dr. Morrow walked into the kitchen and looked at the
astonished faces of the three women. 'I've dismissed the
photographers,' he told them. 'But we have to break the
news to Paul without delay.'

'We certainly do,' replied Rosalind through gritted
teeth. She stood up and fixed her husband with a challenging glare. 'And it will give me the greatest of pleasure.'

St. James' cathedral was a magnificent building set high
on the crest of a hill and commanding a fine view of
Cleveland Bay. Its great interior, vaulted by gleaming timber arches, was overflowing with flowers and filled with
music from a string quartet as Tessa and her father approached.

Tessa felt unexpectedly at ease. All week she'd been
preparing to live out the rest of her days accompanied by
a constant niggling anxiety and haunted by dark, shadowy
regret. Now she felt as if she had clawed her way through
a suffocating, menacing fog and, having reached the surface, she could glimpse enticing snatches of what it was
like to feel at peace with the world. She drew in deep,
steadying breaths of winter air and found, to her surprise,
that she was able to face the task ahead quite calmly.

'Are you feeling all right?' Dr. Morrow asked, guiding

her through the vestry, past a rack of priestly vestments
and towards the door into the main body of the church.
She nodded.

'We'll make this short and sweet,' he added, then
stopped and looked at his daughter. Afternoon sunshine
streamed through a high circular window, highlighting the
gleam of love and resolution in his eyes. 'We'll all survive
this, Tessa,' he said. 'The next few minutes will be hard,
but when they are over, you can be proud of yourself,
possum. You've made a difficult decision, but we all
know you've come to the right conclusion.'

'Yes,' she whispered.

'If I'm honest,' continued John Morrow, 'I must admit
I've suspected for some time that you and Paul didn't feel
quite as intensely or as passionately as you should. I was
afraid that there was something missing in your relationship, but I wasn't prepared to intervene. And as soon as
Isaac came back, well…' Her father slanted her a rueful
smile. 'I guessed Paul didn't really stand much of a
chance—but I didn't know quite what I could do about
it. Of course if I'd had any idea about this other business…' He shook his head sorrowfully.

'It's okay, Dad.' Tessa gave her father's arm a reassuring squeeze. 'Let's get this over with.'

They walked into the flower-bedecked church to face
the waiting guests—friends, relatives, colleagues and curious onlookers—but Tessa knew there was only one face
in the crowd she needed to find. It was only important
that one pair of ears out there heard her father's short
speech.

The string quartet was playing Bach as they approached
the chancel steps, and there were audible gasps from
guests in the front rows. Tessa and John Morrow certainly
looked very different from what the congregation was ex-

pecting. Instead of his formal tuxedo, her father was dressed in a grey business suit, and Tessa had exchanged her beautiful wedding gown for a simple blue wool dress.

Her mother and grandmother were seated, as expected, in the front pew. Rosalind's shoulders were bravely straight, and she held her head high. Tessa could see Alice standing at the back of the church, and for a fraction of a second, she fancied she saw her friend give them the thumbs-up signal.

'Dear family and friends,' her father began solemnly. 'Tessa and I have something to tell you....'

Aware of everyone's eyes on her, Tessa held her head high as John told the congregation that the wedding would not take place. He spoke well, giving no reason for the change of plans except that both Paul and Tessa had arrived at this decision only shortly before the ceremony was to start and that they apologised for the inconvenience and disappointment they had caused so many people.

She looked at the collection of people before her. Some were smiling sadly, nodding their heads and trying to understand, others were weeping or at least dabbing at their eyes. All were stunned, all trying their best to assimilate this astonishing news.

Where was Isaac?

Tessa's eyes scanned the sea of faces again, frantically searching for his tall, dark, aloof figure. Of course she knew he wouldn't come running forward ecstatically to claim her. He was not going to lift her up and swing her in a spectacular slow-motion pirouette before kissing her in front of the entire congregation.

That only happened in the movies.

But she half expected to see him striding, stern-faced, towards Rosalind and demanding to know what was going on.

Then at last she saw him standing to one side of the cathedral in a shadowy recess beneath a stained glass window. He was watching her carefully, his black eyes hooded and secretive, his features a grim mask.

There was no way to tell how he was feeling.

It took ages for everyone to leave. And it took forever to individually thank and apologise to their guests, all of whom wanted to offer sympathy and support. It was gratifying that everyone was so understanding, but Tessa found listening to all their well-meant advice an ordeal. And it was a terribly long time to stand there smiling, nodding and being kissed while she wondered why Isaac had disappeared.

Eventually, people began to drift away. Tessa would have liked to leave, too, if there wasn't one tall, dark person she was still hoping to see.

If Isaac had vanished again, she couldn't think what in sweet heaven she would do with her life. Wearier than she could ever remember feeling, she was waving to a group of old school friends when a dusty black utility truck pulled up at the kerb.

Her heart thumped.

The door opened, and Isaac emerged looking, despite his pale face and strained expression, more handsome than ever in his formal evening suit. He walked stiffly towards her, and Devil bounded over the back of the truck and trotted at his master's feet. Isaac didn't bother to send the dog back.

'Hello, Tessa.'

'Isaac,' she managed to say in a small, choked voice.

'I'm sorry about—the wedding.' His voice, normally rumbling and resonant, sounded flat, without colour.

Tessa nodded. Her palms were damp with sweat, and

her throat was tight with pain. It was agony to stand there and listen to his halting, formal offerings of sympathy, as if he meant no more to her than any of the other guests.

'How are you?' he asked.

She tried to smile, but she was fairly certain the attempt was futile. 'I've felt better.'

Isaac nodded. 'Your father explained this business about Hammond....' He had the grace to look embarrassed, out of his depth.

'It's terrible,' Tessa said quietly. 'But I had already decided not to go ahead with the wedding before I heard the news.'

'You had?' His throat worked.

'I—I didn't love him.' Tessa felt completely exhausted, as if she been climbing a very high mountain and no longer had the strength to struggle to the top. And Isaac wasn't helping. He looked about as in control of the situation as a man sinking in quicksand.

'It was a bit of a shock, the way you called everything off like that at the last minute,' he said gruffly. 'Sure knocked the stuffing out of me. I'd convinced myself that you were just late. Brides are traditionally late for their weddings, aren't they?'

'So the story goes,' replied Tessa. 'It's been a shock all round.'

Was this really her voice sounding so casual, so distanced, when all she wanted to do was throw herself into Isaac's arms?

His face tightened. 'John spoke well.'

She nodded.

'So you're okay?' he asked bleakly.

With her heart swelling to the size of a watermelon, it was a question she couldn't answer twice. 'Isaac, Rosalind told me why you left. She told me what she did—how she lied to you!' She couldn't resist bursting out with her news.

If he had given her the slightest sign, she would have told him more—that she loved him more than ever for his years of painful silence. But the cold, hard set of his mouth and the startled chill of his eyes stifled her impulse.

So instead, she smiled a tiny, tight smile and answered his earlier question. 'I'm feeling very tired—a bit numb.'

The coal black eyes bored straight into hers. 'I'm sorry.' He looked away, and Tessa could see a muscle working in his cheek. When he looked back at her, his eyes glittered. 'I'm sorry if I messed things up for you two, coming back this week. Pretty lousy timing, really.'

Was this all he could say? Tessa bit her lip and bent to scruff Devil in an attempt to hide her dismay. Last night, on the eve of her wedding to another man, she'd offered herself to him, and he'd taken her. The force of his passion had been every bit as violent as her own. Together they'd spun a magic that had carried them to the moon and back.

And he dismissed it as lousy timing.

'Even without this latest news about—the land, Paul and I didn't really have a very good thing going,' she replied as casually as she could. 'My decision didn't really have anything to do with you.'

Only that she belonged to him as the clouds belonged to the wind.

He looked relieved and cracked a crooked grin. 'That's great. Glad to hear it. The last thing I wanted to do was to break up your wedding.'

Then he looked swiftly at the bay. She followed his gaze. A brisk breeze swept from the water, rustling nearby palm fronds and hinting at a cool evening to follow the balmy tropical winter's day. The sun dipped low to the horizon, sending tentacles of gleaming, rosy gold into a purple twilight sky. And nearby, on a shadowy lawn, a carpet of fallen pink bells spread a floral picnic cloth on the grass beneath a tabebuia tree.

'I'll be off, then,' Isaac said suddenly.

'Home?' she asked, her lips trembling.

'Not to your home—to mine. I'd already packed my things so I could make tracks as soon as the wedding was over. I've spoken to your parents. I'll head off back west.'

Isaac, you can't! She wanted to scream. *I've told people I love you. I need to tell you!*

But when he stood before her, fidgeting on the footpath and desperate to get away like a naughty schoolboy held on detention for forgetting his homework, she knew with a terrible certainty that he would not want to hear her message.

'I've made things difficult enough already,' he continued with a shrug of his wide shoulders inside the sleek, black jacket. 'I've got to get away from here so that you and your family can have the time and space you need to get over this and to adjust to—everything.'

'Why the rush?' Tessa demanded in desperation. 'You—you won't get very far today, leaving this late.'

Isaac smiled bleakly and shook his head, as if her pathetic effort to try to hold him wasn't worth any response. Then he stepped closer, his hands reaching for her shoulders.

This was going to be the goodbye kiss? So soon? She blinked back tears of despair, but even so, as he leant towards her she didn't miss the sight of something like torture tightening his features into a fierce grimace.

'You don't have to do this, Isaac,' she whispered.

He froze and stared at her, his dark brows drawn down

in bewilderment. But then he shook his head. His fierce grip on her shoulders almost hurt her.

He planted a brief kiss on her quivering lips and whispered, 'Bye, Tess. I hope things work out for the preschool. At least those little kids will be glad they get to keep you as their teacher. Keep up the great work there.'

Then he swung away, and with a whistle for Devil, strode swiftly to his truck.

CHAPTER ELEVEN

TESSA stood glumly on the footpath wrapped in unbearable misery. In the past week she'd experienced days and nights of emotional turmoil, brief minutes of happiness. Now she could only look forward to long years of wretched loneliness.

It was just too cruel of Isaac to come back into her life for five short days, turn her world inside out and then take off again. How could he possibly leave her when she'd admitted to her parents and Alice that she loved him—had never stopped loving him? And she'd been foolish enough to suspect that he still loved her. Had always loved her.

Just how foolish that tiny hope had been was reinforced by each firm footstep ringing on the pavement as he strode away from her.

His fine words about giving her family space sounded good and even noble. Perhaps he had convinced himself that was why he was leaving. But Tessa was quite sure Isaac was running away from *her*. And this time she knew he would not come back.

Her eyes flooding with tears, Tessa stared at her feet. There was no way she could watch him leave. She heard the slam of his truck door and waited for the other sounds of his departure—the whirr of the ignition, the spurt of the motor roaring to life, the final crunch of tyres on gravel in the gutter before he drove away.

But none of the expected sounds reached her ears.

Instead, she heard two short, sharp whistles. Beside her

165

on the footpath, something moved. She looked down. Devil was still crouched at her heels. In response to the whistles, the dog pricked up his ears, then stood bristling to attention. But he didn't move from her side.

'Devil,' she whispered, 'I think they're your marching orders. You have to go.'

The dog looked at her with his intelligent brown eyes, but he still he didn't move. She heard Isaac's impatient growl.

'C'mon. Here, boy!'

Devil's tail swished, but he didn't budge.

Isaac's footsteps approached. 'What's got into you, you silly mongrel?' he snapped. 'C'mon, Devil! Let's *go!*' he ordered, and grabbed the dog's collar.

Tessa watched in amazement as the eternally faithful Devil refused to obey his master. Isaac tugged at the collar, but the dog strained against him.

'Stupid dog, you've gone crazy on me,' muttered Isaac. He grimaced as he lifted the dog and carried him to the back of the truck. And he scowled at Tessa as he strode once more to the driver's door.

She watched with wretched curiosity as the door slammed again. The ignition was fired, but before the tyres could rotate, Devil bounded over the side of the vehicle and trotted back, panting at Tessa's feet.

'You're in deep trouble,' she told the dog as the engine died and Isaac glared at them. In spite of her desperate heartache, her lips itched to smile at the uncharacteristic behaviour. Devil never disobeyed his master! But she managed to look stern as Isaac marched to the footpath, fury darkening his already grim features.

'What's got into him?' she asked.

'Heaven only knows. Are you feeding him something?'

'Hardly,' replied Tessa, opening her hands and holding

them out to prove her innocence. Then, in a totally un-
deserved act of betrayal, Devil sent a long, pink tongue
curling up to lick at her hand. Tessa tried to stifle a wild
urge to laugh hysterically. 'I swear it, Isaac. I haven't fed
him.'

'Looks like I'll just have to tie him up.' Isaac strode
over to the back of his truck and returned with a leather
lead.

Hopeless and heart-weary, Tessa watched as he
snapped the lead to Devil's collar. So much trouble to get
away from her as quickly as possible! This time there
would be no escape for Devil. Isaac would make certain
they got away.

'Your dog has more intelligence than you do, Isaac,' a
shrill voice called suddenly from behind them.

Tessa spun around. Lydia had reached the bottom of
the cathedral steps and was hobbling towards them, leaning on a walking stick. 'Grandma, I thought you'd gone
home.'

'Not yet, dear,' replied Lydia. 'I was helping your
mother with the flowers. We've left some for the church,
but we've arranged for the others to be sent to the hospital.'

'Oh, that's a good idea,' said Tessa. Her eyes swung to
Isaac, who was poised for flight, his dog reined in tightly
at his side.

'I was just making my farewells,' Isaac told Lydia.

'I know, you silly man.' With her head on one side,
Lydia fixed Isaac with a beady eye. She reminded Tessa
of a small, shrewd bird. 'I meant what I said, Isaac. Your
dog has more sense than you do.'

'How so?' asked Isaac, sounding bored, looking impatient.

'He knows your place is here on the footpath beside

Tessa. Not galloping off into the wild west again like some lonesome cowboy. You shouldn't be leaving without Tessa, at any rate.'

Isaac looked stunned.

Tessa felt ill. 'Grandma, please,' she said.

But Lydia continued to fix Isaac with eyes sharp as gimlets. 'Rosalind's told me all about this unfortunate affair. How she forced you to leave Tessa last time, Isaac. And she knows she made a terrible mistake. The whole family owes you an apology. But don't make a worse mistake now, my boy.' She shook a papery thin hand at him.

Isaac stared at her. His hand gripping the lead was white with tension, and his mouth had reduced to a thin, bleak line.

'Rosalind was devious in her efforts to keep you apart. But, if it's necessary, *I* will be just as devious to bring you two together,' Lydia concluded. 'Blind Fred can see that you two belong together.'

Tessa's father approached. 'Can I help you to the car, Mum?' he asked, after nodding briefly to Tessa and Isaac.

'Just a minute, John,' Lydia ordered him imperiously, then she faced Isaac once more. 'I won't be the first one who's spoken the truth and been called a fool, but I don't meddle to cause trouble.'

'Mum,' interrupted Dr. Morrow once more, 'I think we should leave these two young people....' He shook his head at Isaac and raised an eyebrow in exasperation.

Lydia accepted her son-in-law's arm with good grace but turned one last time to glare at Isaac. 'Be warned.' She shot the words at him. 'If you make a mess of things today, you'll have the rest of your life to regret it. And believe me, a life can last a long, long time.'

Her chest painfully tight, Tessa watched her father patiently guide Lydia to the waiting vehicle. If she'd been able to breathe, she might have raced after them. She had never felt so embarrassed.

She turned to Isaac and shook her head. 'I apologise for my grandmother. I guess she figures that at her age she can say what she likes and get away with it. It seems she fancies she's some kind of matchmaker.'

'It does indeed,' he responded grimly.

Two of Tessa's fingers twisted into her hair. Never had she felt so frightened. Isaac was hovering impatiently on the footpath, eager to get away. He was about to leave her forever. If only she were clever enough, she might be able to find something witty to say to detain him. There were so many questions she needed to ask. She knew why he'd stayed away, but why had he come back?

'How about it?' he asked softly, reaching out to disentangle her fingers from her hair.

Tessa swallowed a lump of something prickly in her throat. He was looking at her, and his eyes held a frightening mixture of sadness and exhaustion. But his mouth was smiling. His beautiful, sensuous mouth. His smile was uncertain, boyish.

Her heart seemed to freeze mid-beat. 'How about what?' she asked.

'How about we take this faithless hound somewhere and have a—talk.'

'You—you really want to?'

'Yes. I really want to.'

Somehow she answered calmly. He was offering her an olive branch, and she wanted the whole orchard, so she wasn't about to let go and do cartwheels all over the pavement.

But she felt as if she could, easily.

* * *

The purple twilight had merged into the dark navy of early evening as they drove down the hill away from the cathedral.

'Would you like to go somewhere for a meal or will we hit the beach?' Isaac asked.

Tessa glanced at his exquisitely tailored formal suit. 'You're not exactly dressed for the beach, but I'm sure Devil would prefer a run on the sand.'

'That no-good mongrel's received far too much attention today,' Isaac growled in mock dismay. 'Still, I rather fancy some fish and chips on the beach—like old times. How does that sound?'

'Delicious. I'm actually very hungry. I feel like I haven't eaten for days.'

'Knowing you, you probably haven't.'

They stopped at the local fish shop and bought their meal wrapped in paper. Isaac picked up a couple of cans of drink from the shop next door. By the time they reached the beach at Rowes Bay, night cloaked the sea, the sand and the sky in black velvet. The lights of Magnetic Island winked at them across the water. The night air was crisp and cool.

'There's a rug in the back of the truck somewhere,' Isaac told her, and after rummaging around, he produced it. 'I'm afraid there'll be a few dog hairs, but it'll help keep the sand out of our food.'

For a while they ate in silence. The savoury smell of the hot chips had awakened Tessa's appetite at first, but as she settled on the rug beside a sprawling Isaac, she was nervous—so nervous that she could only toy with her food. Her future depended on getting this conversation right, but she could think of nothing to say.

'You wanted to talk?' she asked tentatively.

'I did,' answered Isaac gruffly. He snapped the top off

a can and offered it to her. She shook her head. 'But it's damn hard to get the words out.' He took a deep swig.

She bit her lip. He probably wanted to find a way to tell her gently that they had no future, that he didn't love her. Why else had he been in such a hurry to leave before Lydia accosted him? She consoled herself with the thought that Isaac hadn't tried to deny Lydia's claim that they belonged together.

'There's so much that we *could* talk about,' she began. The shadows on his face made his expression unreadable. It would help if she could gauge his reaction.

Isaac scratched his head. 'There are lots of things— Lydia's comments, for starters,' he agreed, but then he abruptly wrapped the fish and chips up and thrust them aside. He moved across the rug towards her. She could just make out his dark eyes, inches from hers.

Talk about moonlight madness. They had desperate problems to sort out. Tessa knew they should have been talking, but with Isaac this close, words dissolved and were replaced by the much stronger need to touch and to be held.

He must have shared that need, for suddenly, silently, he reached for her.

She should have protested. Minutes from now Isaac could be walking away from her yet again. She certainly should not have been so weak as to melt towards him, her lips parting in readiness.

But when had she ever been strong enough to resist Isaac?

He touched her cheek, and she leant into the curve of his hand, moving her lips against his palm. His thumb traced the outline of her mouth as if committing its shape and texture to memory. And then his lips joined his thumb, grazing her mouth softly, teasing her, tempting her. He tasted salty. Delicious. With tantalising slowness, his lips trailed over her face, pressing her eyelids closed, caressing the tip of her nose and nuzzling her ears.

Oh, how she loved the feel and the taste of Isaac. His touch sent coils of heat spiralling through her body.

Her hands slipped behind his neck, and she threaded urgent fingers through his silky hair. She held him against her, her small teeth nipping at the soft insides of his bottom lip, pleading a deeper intimacy.

The evening seemed to cradle them with comforting darkness and hushed, soothing sounds. Just metres away, little waves crashed onto the shore with soft sighs. This was a different Isaac—tender, gentle. A loving Isaac? Was it only last night that she'd been in his arms? Then he'd been fiercely passionate.

The memory chilled her. She stiffened in his embrace. Passion hadn't helped her solve any problems with Isaac in the past, and flirting with passion was hardly going to help now.

She pulled away from him and sat up.

'Tess, what's the matter?' he asked, lying with his empty arms outstretched. He grabbed at her playfully and tried to pull her onto his chest. She resisted.

'No, Isaac. Seducing me is not going to sort anything out.'

'Seducing you?' Isaac laughed. 'Me seducing you?' he repeated. 'If anyone around here is proficient in the art of seduction—'

Tessa could feel her face burning. 'I think we've established that physically we're—compatible,' she responded somewhat formally.

Isaac hauled himself into a sitting position. 'Yes, I think we could consider that fact established,' he gently mocked her. 'Although we haven't had a lot of time to study that truism in enough depth to come to any firm conclusions.'

The moon drifted out from behind a cloud and lit a silvery pathway across the bay. As its light reached Isaac, Tessa almost moaned aloud at the masculine perfection it revealed.

'Oh, Isaac. Let's not be flippant. I'm afraid this has been the worst day of my life.'

There was a long moment of silence.

'Ditto,' he said at last, his voice suddenly bitter.

'So you've been miserable, too?' Her heart shouldn't be skittering with anything approaching hope, but it seemed to have a will of its own. She watched as he stared out to sea and the moon outlined his rugged profile with a silvery finger.

'Sitting in that church today, waiting for you to arrive, was sheer hell, Tess. I felt like I was standing on the brink of a cliff watching you fall away from me—forever.' He turned to stare at her, his eyes burning with a frightening intensity. 'I knew you'd been crying about something. I was damn sure you shouldn't be marrying Hammond. But I had no idea you would actually call the wedding off.'

'I guess not.'

'I started imagining all kinds of wild scenes. I could see myself running up to the church door and blocking your way if you tried to come down the aisle,' Isaac said. Then he jumped to his feet and turned towards her, his expression once more fierce. 'Or—or I could picture that part in the ceremony when the priest wants to know any reason why these two should not be joined in holy matrimony. I was thinking of leaping to my feet and yelling, *Yes, I do! She was making mad, passionate love to me last night!*'

Tessa's mouth fell open. 'That would have been effective.'

Isaac's grin was fleeting.

'Let's go for a walk,' he said, offering her a hand up. 'If you don't want me to ravish you senseless here on the beach, I'll look the other way while you get your stockings off. I'm getting rid of these shoes.'

Obediently, she slipped her pantihose down and tried not to think about being ravished senseless by Isaac.

Isaac rolled his trousers above his ankles and unhooked Devil. While the dog darted in blissful circles around them, he took Tessa's hand. They began to walk towards the distant sprinkling of lights at Cape Pallarenda.

It was an idyllic setting. The sand beneath their feet was still warm from the day's sunshine. To their left, palm trees and whispering casuarinas hid them from the road, and at their right, the sea, protected by offshore reefs, hummed and lapped gently. Surely such a scene was designed for a memorable romantic interlude.

But how would she remember this evening, wondered Tessa desperately as she walked beside Isaac. Her mind clung to his comments about waiting in the church as a drowning man clings to a life raft.

Perhaps?

Isaac seemed lost in his thoughts as they walked. His thumb circled her hand with absent-minded, leisurely strokes.

Tessa looked across the sea, and her eyes caught a streak of bright light on the far horizon. 'Look—a falling star!' she exclaimed, pointing quickly.

'Make a wish, Tess,' Isaac urged softly.

Tessa glanced at him nervously. 'A wish?' she repeated, her voice thin and shaky.

'What do you wish for?'

Isaac was staring at her so intently, Tessa lowered her eyes. There was no way she could share the details of her foolish fantasies with him. 'Oh, I guess my wishes are the same as most people's,' she murmured vaguely.

From somewhere up the beach, Devil barked at a piece of driftwood. Tessa grabbed the opportunity to distract Isaac. 'I wonder if dogs make wishes?'

But it seemed he was determined to continue. 'I made a wish a long time ago,' he told her.

'You—you did?' Tessa stammered. Isaac was still staring at her, his eyes glistening. Surely those weren't tears?

'I don't know why I persisted in believing that my wish might come true when every reality in my life showed me it was clearly impossible. But then, it would have seemed such a simple ambition to most people. Perhaps it's because of the kind of childhood I had, but I wished for...' Isaac paused and smiled a little, broken smile.

Tessa's heart pounded, and she pressed her hands against her chest in an attempt to quieten its savage beating.

'My wish was for a house and a garden full of children—lots of children—' He reached out a shaking hand to gently brush her cheek. He was staring at her fiercely. Sweet heaven! There *were* tears. 'I wished for all that and one more, most important thing—my golden girl.'

Tessa's throat ached with a swelling of undistilled emotion. She tried to speak, but no sound emerged. Then eventually she croaked, 'Oh, Isaac, that—that's not so impossible, is it?'

'Only you can tell me the answer to that, sweet girl.'

'Isaac,' she said. 'You must know how I feel about you.' She raised shaky fingers to his cheek. 'It's my dream, too. It's all I've ever wanted, ever dared to hope for. Your dream is not only possible, as far as I'm concerned, it's compulsory.'

'Tess.' Isaac drew her to him roughly and buried his face in her hair. 'I don't know why I was trying to run away from you again, because the truth is that I can't go on without you, my darling. Without you I'm rootless, unable to grow.'

Tessa clung to him, her heart soaring. He held her tenderly and kissed her hair, her ears, her nose and her eyelids.

'I love you, Tessa,' he said.

'This is so hard to believe,' she cried against his chest. 'You really love me?'

'I really love you.'

'You've loved me all this time?'

'Since I was twelve years old and I first woke up in your home. You brought me a tray with milk and biscuits.'

'I remember that.' Tessa laughed. 'You looked so dark and wild, and I was a little frightened of you.' Now, in the moonlight, he still looked dark and wild, but so sexy, she felt limp with longing.

'And you looked beautiful. I was bewitched. I'd never seen anything so delicate. I fell in love at once with your golden hair and your enchanting smile.'

'That was a long, long time ago,' she whispered against his shoulder. 'I've never stopped loving you, Isaac.'

'Thank God, Tess,' he breathed, caressing her hair and her face and her neck. 'And now you're more beautiful than ever. A beautiful person—on the inside as well as the outside.'

Arms entwined, they lingered along the moonlit beach, in no hurry to end this precious moment.

'Can you imagine how I felt when I learned you were engaged to be married?' he asked.

'Is—is that why you came back?'

'I never admitted it even to myself,' Isaac said. 'I wasn't going to come here at all. I told myself that your wedding was what I wanted—to see you committed elsewhere so that I could get on with my life. Then I decided I was just coming to see your father. But then, when I did see you again and you threw your gorgeous self into my arms, I—I thought my heart would break.'

'It might have been something like how I felt when you disappeared,' said Tessa, her voice breaking on a sob.

Isaac nodded and sighed. 'I worked so hard over in Western Australia. I worked hard to forget you *and* I worked to prove myself to you.'

'You never had to prove anything to me, Isaac.'

'To Rosalind, then.'

Tessa sighed. It would take a while to adjust to the shock of Rosalind's confession, but she knew that eventually she would be able to forgive her mother. 'Mum feels terrible about what she did,' she said softly.

'I'm sure she does. She's not such a bad old stick.'

'You can say that now,' Tessa laughed. 'Now that I'm yours forever.'

A roar of triumph burst from Isaac's lips, and he lifted Tessa and spun her round and round. They both sank breathless onto the sand in a happy, laughing heap. Devil came bounding over to them to check they were all right, then licked them thoroughly before trotting away again.

'Forever, Tess. What a magic word!' Isaac kissed the back of her neck. 'Honestly, I can see things a bit more from Rosalind's point of view now. I'm sure I'll be checking out the credentials of any pimply youths that come snooping around our daughter.'

'Oh, yes,' mused Tessa, reaching up to undo Isaac's necktie. 'These children you mentioned in passing. How many were you contemplating?' She slipped the tie from beneath Isaac's collar, tucked it into his coat pocket and began to unbutton his shirt.

'If you keep that up my girl, I'll be incapable of contemplating anything but your delectable body. There's a good chance you will be eternally pregnant.'

Tessa shot him a cheeky smile. 'If you want me to keep my figure—' Then her face grew serious. She dropped her hands into her lap. 'I guess your home will be in Western Australia.'

He nodded. 'I'm pretty firmly entrenched there. I'm based in Perth now. It's actually a beautiful city.' He frowned. 'Will that be a problem?'

'No,' she said slowly. 'I was just thinking about the children at the preschool.'

Isaac sat forward and stared out to sea. 'Yeah,' he sighed. 'That is something that deserves some thought. With all the publicity this whole escapade will attract, I doubt the school will fold. But still, you can't just abandon them.'

'No,' Tessa agreed. 'Although I'm fairly confident I can find someone to take my place.'

'That's good. No need to rush. You've got to make sure it's someone really suitable.'

Tessa smiled. 'Another Mother Teresa type?'

'Ouch.' Isaac's face twisted in a rueful smile. 'I can see I'll have to make up for that smart comment. At least the shed renovations are taken care of.'

'The what?' Tessa stared at Isaac in bewilderment.

'Oh, it's nothing, really, just some shares I had that paid out well last week. So I organised for a new roof for the preschool, properly lined walls—that sort of thing. Of course the renovations can't happen till this whole issue's resolved, but the money's still there.'

'Isaac!' cried Tessa, throwing her arms around him again. 'You're a closet philanthropist! Next you'll be wanting to foster all of the children.'

Isaac chuckled. 'Now that thought has crossed my mind.'

'Oh, Isaac, I love you.'

Tessa reached out once more for his shirt, and as each button was released at her touch, she bent to kiss his dark chest. Her tongue curled into the covering of crisp hair. 'Where's that picnic rug of yours?' she asked breathlessly.

'Seduction again, Queen Tess?' Isaac asked with a deep, rumbling laugh as he lifted her effortlessly.

'Yes,' she whispered as he carried her across the shadowy sand. 'I want you to seduce me, Isaac.'

'Tell me more,' he murmured huskily as he lowered her onto the rug. He knelt above her, clasping her hips between his knees. 'What else does my lady require?'

Tessa gasped. Isaac loomed over her, and suddenly she no longer felt in charge of her mind or her body. She could only think of total, blissful surrender. 'No other special requests tonight,' she said, smiling and wriggling seductively beneath his heated gaze.

'No?'

She could hear the faint swish and splash of the sea as it ebbed and flowed. Isaac lowered his head and kissed her with mesmerising gentleness, and Tessa knew she was floating on happiness. Then one thought that had been bothering her resurfaced. 'Actually there is one special request.'

'Whatever you wish,' he said softly, and trailed more kisses across her cheek and down her neck.

A delighted shudder rippled through Tessa. But she resisted the urge to abandon herself immediately to the heady sensations Isaac always aroused in her. 'It's actually one thing I *don't* want,' she said quietly. 'I don't want to get married.'

'You don't?' Isaac straightened. 'But, Tessa, I thought I—we— What do you think I've been talking about?'

'Darling,' she said, reaching up to caress his lips with her fingers, 'everything you've said tonight has been absolutely perfect, but we haven't actually talked about marriage, as in ceremonies, and it's just that I've had rather an overdose of the whole wedding business lately. I can't face the thought of another ceremony just now.'

'I guess I can believe that,' Isaac agreed after a few moments' silence. 'So you're asking me to—to wait?' His lopsided smile wavered.

'Well—not wait, exactly. No! No more waiting, Isaac. I couldn't bear it.' She pulled his mouth down to hers and kissed him deeply, hungrily.

When at last they parted, he said shakily, 'I believe you. So what are you suggesting?'

'You're doing this deliberately, aren't you? These days people—well, no one calls it living in sin any more.'

She heard his deep chuckle.

'Do you mind?' she whispered. 'I really am desperate to be your wife, darling—when we've had time to think about exactly what kind of wedding *we* want.'

'You're lucky I'm in the mood for granting your wishes tonight,' said Isaac, but then he grinned. 'We might as well be living in sin, because we'll most certainly be living with Devil.'

Tessa laughed, then lay still, her imagination captured completely by the thought of living with Isaac. Waking each day to see him beside her. Sharing her hopes with him. Spending nights lost in a world of bliss in his arms.

'Now for those other requests.' His deep voice broke into her reverie.

'I thought you'd forgotten,' she teased.

He dropped a quick kiss onto her laughing mouth. 'Can you remind me?'

'I think my request had something to do with seduction,' she answered with breathless impatience.

'And my response will have more to do with love—with just how much I love you,' he murmured against her neck.

'Oh, yes, Isaac. Tell me again about that.'

EPILOGUE

FOURTEEN months later...

As the sun moved over the Kimberley ranges in the remote north-west of Australia, the steep limestone walls of the gorge below were transformed from gold to deep red. Within the cabin of a helicopter travelling above the gorge, Tessa, her parents and Alice gazed in awe at the beauty of the wilderness beneath them. Their craft hovered over ancient cliffs carved into fantastic towering shapes by the Fitzroy River, then swooped low over steep banks topped by river gums and yellow flowering Leichhardt trees.

Alice reached over and squeezed Tessa's hand.

'Tess, I can't believe it,' she shouted over the chop, chop, chop of the rotating blades. 'This country is absolutely out of this world. I had no idea it was so incredibly beautiful.'

Tessa nodded, too thrilled to speak. Six months earlier, she had driven through the Kimberley region, travelling with Isaac from Broome along the Great Northern Highway, but this was her first view of the incredible collection of ranges and gorges from the air.

Deep within the gorge below, the river wound its way, depositing sand every so often to form generous stretches of beach. And it was towards one of these areas that the helicopter finally descended.

As the noise of the motor finally chugged to silence, the pilot opened the cabin door, and Rosalind and John moved forwards.

Alice gave Tessa's hand another excited squeeze. 'You look so happy, Tessa. You're positively luminous.'

'I've never felt so relaxed, so absolutely certain about what I'm going to do,' Tessa responded, sending her friend a bright-eyed smile. 'I know this dress is totally unsuitable for the wilderness, but I couldn't possibly get married in anything else.'

'I'm so glad you're still wearing this beautiful gown,' Alice reassured her, 'even if absolutely nothing else about your wedding is—the same.'

'I can see them!' Dr. Morrow's voice called excitedly from the ground. 'I can see Isaac.'

Tessa's heart leapt in her chest as she jumped out of her seat and rushed to the cabin door. 'Where? Where is he?' she cried. 'Let me see him.' Lifting her long skirt high, she prepared to dash down the flimsy metal stairs.

'Hold on, sweetheart,' her father chided her. 'Here, take my hand before you fall. Isaac will want you here in one piece.'

With her father's strong grip supporting her, Tessa almost leapt to the ground. 'Where is Isaac?' she called as soon as she reached the bottom.

'Should you be speaking to him before the ceremony?' queried Rosalind.

'Oh, Mum,' sighed Tessa impatiently. 'This is our style of wedding, remember? We're breaking with a few traditions.'

'Of course, dear. I'm sorry,' replied her mother contritely. 'This is your day.'

Tessa would have paused to give her mother a swift hug if she hadn't just seen Isaac striding towards her from the riverbank. 'Isaac!' she cried, lifting her skirts and rushing towards him. How splendid he looked—so tall and impossibly handsome in his dark suit and crisp, white shirt, his hair raven black.

'Tess.'

She hurled herself into his arms, and her cheek met the smooth cloth of his jacket and the strong, muscled chest beneath. Then her body was enfolded in his arms as he crushed her tightly to him. 'Oh, Isaac I've missed you.'

'I've missed you, too, my darling,' he murmured into her ear, his lips brushing her with a deliciously feather-light touch.

'A week was far too long to be away from you,' she whispered.

'I've hated being apart, too,' he agreed. 'But now you're here. And I'm so glad you're happy to be married here. For me, this is the most special place in the world. And I have everything ready for our wedding. Let me look at you.' Isaac drew back and held Tessa at arm's length. 'Oh, darling,' he whispered. 'You're wearing the gold heart.'

'Of course,' she smiled.

Then his dark eyes gleamed as they continued to travel slowly over her, taking in her glowing face, the bouquet of pale pink rosebuds that had miraculously avoided being crushed in his embrace and the exquisite gown with its dreamy train floating behind her in the afternoon breeze. 'Are you real? You look like a fairy-tale princess,' he whispered, his throat working rapidly.

Tessa laughed. 'That's the whole idea. I'm supposed to.' Then she stepped towards him again. 'But, darling, the best part is that yes, this *is* real, and you're my man, and I'm here to marry you.'

'At last,' sighed Isaac happily, linking her arm through his and turning to the riverbank. He pointed to a massive, gnarled tree with an unusually thick trunk and wide, spreading branches. 'This is the boab tree I was telling you about.'

'It's beautiful.'

'And it's also regarded as very special by my Aboriginal friends in this district. That's why I want to be married in its shade. The elders have given us special permission to come in here.'

As Isaac led her forwards, he called over his shoulder to Tessa's parents and Alice. 'Come and meet my best man, David Windjana, and the rest of the gang.'

The members of the gang, their faces expectant and split by wide smiles, were waiting in the shade of a cluster of river gums near the boab tree. There was a bush priest, who had been flown in especially for the ceremony, and several of Isaac and Tessa's friends from Perth, plus a group of the Aborigines who had befriended Isaac when he first came to the region eight years earlier. One of them, a tall, impressively handsome young man, stepped forwards and extended his hand to Tessa.

'It's wonderful to see you again,' he told her, gripping her hand firmly.

'It's great to be back, David, and you must meet my parents and best friend, Alice.'

After Isaac had helped with all the introductions, David was still staring at Tessa, his dark eyes absorbed by her smiling face and bright hair. 'You look better than ever, Tessa—more beautiful than anyone I've ever seen in the movies. No wonder Isaac's been chafing at the bit. I'm so glad you're going to put this poor fella out of his misery at last.'

Everybody laughed.

A cloudless blue sky spread like a blessing above the assembled group, and towering red cliffs stood guard. A few yards away, a rough bush table groaned under the weight of baskets of food and ice buckets full of drinks. Folding canvas chairs were arranged nearby, and there was plenty of evidence that very soon there would be a happy celebration.

'Let's have a wedding!' cried David.

Without delay, everyone gathered in a circle in the shade of the huge tree and the priest began the ceremony. Tessa's eyes were shining as she offered Isaac her hand along with her favourite lines from the Book of Ruth. 'Wherever you go, I will go. Wherever you live, I will live. Your people will be my people, and your God will be my God.'

For several moments after she finished speaking, Isaac stood transfixed. His eyes held hers until David leant over and handed him a plain gold band. Smiling his thanks, Isaac took Tessa's fluttering hand in his and slipped the ring onto her finger. Then he quickly drew a piece of paper from his coat pocket.

He flashed her a boyish grin of apology. 'I don't want to get these words wrong,' he said. 'I've combined something from Shakespeare with my own words.' But he only glanced briefly at the paper before shoving it into his pocket. Taking Tessa into his arms, he told her tenderly, 'Tessa, hear my soul speak. The very instant I saw you, did my heart fly to your service. And there, I promise, will it remain for the rest of my days.'

Then the circle of misty-eyed well-wishers gathered closer as the priest finally pronounced the happy couple man and wife. And a radiant Tessa raised her face to receive her first kiss from her husband.

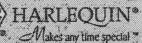

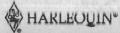

Harlequin Romance®

Coming Next Month

#3615 BACHELOR IN NEED Jessica Steele
Jegar Urquart needed Fennia's help in looking after his niece while
her parents were in hospital. Jegar clearly found Fennia attractive…
but while she could answer Jegar's need for a live-in nanny, Fennia
felt she must resist slipping into the role of live-in lover as well!

The Marriage Pledge

#3616 A MOTHER FOR MOLLIE Barbara McMahon
Patrick O'Shaunnessy can't help Shelby unravel her past—he's too
busy trying to run his investigative business and care for his little
girl! So Shelby suggests a temporary marriage: she'll look after his
daughter while he works for her. But Shelby starts wanting a more
permanent arrangement….

Beaufort Brides

#3617 THE FAITHFUL BRIDE Rebecca Winters
Years after Wade had called off their wedding, Janet found out why:
a friend had told him she was having an affair! Now Janet wanted
another wedding. She knew Wade would have no doubt of her
innocence come the honeymoon! But first she had to convince
him she was a bride worth trusting….

White Weddings

#3618 HIS DESERT ROSE Liz Fielding
When Prince Hassan al Rashid drew the world's media attention to
the abduction of well-known foreign correspondent Rose Fenton,
he also lost his heart. And, kidnapped by Hassan, Rose was
surprised to find that beneath the designer suit lay the heart of a
true desert prince!